Cold hard steel

Quickly and silently, the team took up ambush positions along the east side of the trail and settled back into the bush. The enemy pointman showed up a few minutes later, his AK cradled carelessly in his arms as he hurried along.

Obviously, this was one NVA who wasn't expecting to find Americans in his particular part of Laos. The main body followed closely on his heels, and they were no more alert than their pointman had been.

Through his field glasses, Reese saw the drag man in a dark khaki uniform walking up the trail with his AK slung over his shoulder. Reese caught Kowalski's eye and drew his finger across his own throat.

Kowalski nodded and slipped his K-Bar knife from the sheath taped upside down on the left strap of his assault harness and silently stepped out of the bush behind the NVA, the K-Bar held low in his hand.

HATCHET

SPECTRE

Knox Gordon

A GOLD EAGLE BOOK FROM

WORLDWIDE®

TORONTO • NEW YORK • LONDON
AMSTERDAM • PARIS • SYDNEY • HAMBURG
STOCKHOLM • ATHENS • TOKYO • MILAN
MADRID • WARSAW • BUDAPEST • AUCKLAND

First edition June 1992

ISBN 0-373-63205-3

Special thanks and acknowledgment to
Michael Kasner for his contribution to this work.

SPECTRE

Printed in U.S.A.

SPECTRE

FOREWARD

One of the most important innovations in modern tactical air support that emerged from the Vietnam War experience was the fixed-wing gunship with side-firing weapons. Like many successful ideas, the concept was simple, but its application took time.

The first application of a side-firing machine gun to a ground-attack plane came in 1927. Although it worked well, the Army Air Corps wasn't interested in the radical concept. In World War II Lieutenant Colonel G. C. MacDonald twice tried to get permission to mount side-firing machine guns and bazookas on observation aircraft and was twice turned down.

In the early sixties the Air Force was trying to improve its tactical support of ground troops, and MacDonald's concept arose again. After overcoming intense official disapproval, it was given limited testing. The project languished until Captain Ron Terry, a fighter pilot recently returned from a combat tour in Vietnam, was assigned to the project. His tests conclusively proved that the side-mounted weapons worked well. In late 1964 he was sent to South Vietnam to try the weapons in combat.

The first fixed-wing gunships were converted World War II C-47 Goonie Birds armed with four .30-caliber machine guns firing out of the left side of the plane.

The old Browning machine guns were soon replaced with three 7.62 mm, multibarrel SUU-11A minigun Gatling. The gunships became an instant battlefield success.

At first the AC-47s were known as "Puff the Magic Dragon" after the popular Peter, Paul and Mary song, because tongues of flame seemed to leap from the gunship to the ground when it fired. Later they took the radio call sign "Spooky," and the name stuck. Dozens of American units and Special Forces camps in danger of being overrun owed their survival to Spooky's timely intervention.

The AC-47s worked well, but they were old and worn-out. To replace them, several Korean War C-119 Flying Boxcars were converted into gunships. The resulting AC-119 Shadows were a vast improvement over the old Spookies, but still were not exactly what was needed.

The gunship reached its apex in Vietnam with the introduction of the AC-130A Spectre in 1968. Converted from the four-turboprop Lockheed C-130 Hercules assault transport, Spectre was the answer for a modern, state-of-the-art, deadly gunship.

After its introduction, the Spectre gunship ruled the night skies over Laos and Cambodia and caused great concern to the North Vietnamese and their Russian advisers. The North Vietnamese desperately needed to know how to counter it, and the Russians wanted to examine one to see if it could be as useful to their tactical air support arm as it was to ours.

1

High over Laos—July 23, 1968

It was 0323 hours. The moon was full and the sky over the part of southeastern Laos code-named Steel Tiger was cloudless. It was a perfect night for North Vietnamese army supply trucks to make a high-speed run down the Ho Chi Minh Trail. Unknown to the NVA, however, a prototype high-tech American gunship, the AC-130A Spectre, was prowling the skies above them, looking for targets.

The Spectre's upper surface was camouflaged in two shades of mat-green and tan, and its bottom was painted glossy black. The gunship was devoid of national markings and bore only a dull red five-digit number on its tall tail. On its nose was painted the figure of the Grim Reaper with the name Spectre written in red below it.

In the cockpit the pilot, Lieutenant Colonel Dusty Rhodes, put the four-engine gunship into a sharp left-hand pylon turn. Below him, a hard-packed laterite road snaked across the plain at the foot of a chain of small hills. The road kept tightly to the wood line and was thus shielded from aerial observation. However, the FLIR, a Forward-Looking Infrared sensor, had detected infrared radiation patterns that indicated six large trucks were moving down the road at about forty miles an hour.

At his station outside the sensor booth Major Norman "Nails" Hammer, the Spectre's fire control officer, bent over his monitors, studying the pictures sent from the sensor stations. Using a control stick, he centered the weapon's cross hairs over the lead truck in the convoy. If they blasted it to wreckage, the rest would be bottled up and could be destroyed at their leisure.

He clicked his throat mike. "Nail 'em," he told the pilot.

In the converted cargo bay in the rear of the gunship a 20 mm multibarrel Vulcan cannon opened up on the target with a roar. A brief finger of fire shot from the left side of the sharply banked gunship and raced for the ground. Where the flaming finger touched down destruction followed. The lead NVA truck was carrying ammunition supplies, and it erupted with a ball of flame that lit up the night sky.

Hammer shifted his sights to the last truck and keyed his throat mike again. "Okay, let's bottle 'em up and kill 'em."

The Vulcan growled again, and the last truck exploded with a roar, blocking the trucks in between the two blazing wrecks. Hammer centered the entire convoy in his sights. "Go for it!" he ordered. "Fire all four Vulcans."

What had been a single, brief finger of fire now became a four-fingered fist that hammered the convoy into oblivion. Multiple flashes lit the sky as the trucks' high-explosive cargoes detonated. After a few seconds, Hammer keyed his mike. "Okay, Dusty, that takes care of that bunch. Let's find some more."

The Spectre's pilot leveled out of his banking turn, and the sensor operators went back to their screens. All of them knew that the Ho Chi Minh trail would never be the same....

ALTHOUGH THE FAMOUS North Vietnamese supply route into the battleground of South Vietnam was called the Ho Chi Minh Trail, it wasn't a trail. In some places it was a paved two-lane superhighway. In other places it was merely a potholed, muddy track winding through the jungle as it snaked from North Vietnam through the supposedly neutral nations of Laos and Cambodia to fan out at several points along the South Vietnamese border. Whatever the surface of the road, however, it was the major supply route for the North Vietnamese army. Russian- and Chinese-built trucks carried an average of over three thousand tons of supplies a day to the South during the dry season when the route was open.

The successful interdiction of this supply route was widely seen as the key to defeating the North Vietnamese army by cutting off the supplies needed to wage war in South Vietnam. The problem, of course, wasn't as simple as that, because nothing in the Vietnam War was simple. As always, shortsighted politics were involved in what should have been a purely military problem. Since most of the Ho Chi Minh Trail was in the "neutral" territory of Laos and Cambodia, the sensible military solution of sending in a ground force to cut the Trail wasn't a politically acceptable option.

Instead, the U.S. Air Force was given the mission of conducting a clandestine war from the skies over the Trail. Its job was to destroy the supply trucks, and it expended much effort toward this goal. But the Air Force really didn't have aircraft suitable for this mission. Several different planes were used over the Trail with varying success—high-flying B-52 bombers, Night Intruder B-57s and Korean War vintage A-1 Skyraiders. They all killed trucks, but not in large enough numbers to make a real difference in the flow of vital military supplies to the South.

What was needed was a specialized night-attack aircraft. When Air Force personnel saw the success of the AC-47 Spooky gunships in South Vietnam, they thought they had finally found the right tool to do the job. When Spooky was sent out over the Trail, however, it ran into something it hadn't faced in South Vietnam: heavy antiaircraft fire. The Spookies worked well, but they paid a heavy price because they flew too low and too slow to escape the antiaircraft fire. Having proven the concept, the Air Force went back to the drawing board to design a Super Spooky—the AC-130A Spectre gunship.

Like the famous AC-47 Spooky gunship that had preceded it, the Spectre was a converted transport plane, in this case a Lockheed C-130 Hercules. The high-wing, four-turboprop Herky Bird was the workhorse of the Vietnam War and the world's most successful assault transport plane. Much faster than the World War II era AC-47s, it could fly higher and carry a far greater payload of fuel, weapons and ammunition.

Where the Spooky had carried only three 7.62 mm miniguns, the Spectre was a state-of-the-art flying battleship. Four 7.62 mm MXU-470 miniguns plus four 20 mm M-31 multibarrel Vulcan cannons had been fitted to it. Spooky pilots had sighted their weapons through a Navy Mark 20 Mod 4 gunsight salvaged from a Skyraider and bolted to the left side of the pilot's cockpit framing, but the Spectre had a full fire control system built in, including a ballistics computer.

And where Spooky had depended on the pilot's trained eyes to find targets, Spectre carried the latest high-tech sensors and detection equipment. A Forward-Looking Infrared system (FLIR), Moving Target Indicator radar (MTI), Low-Light Television (LLTV) and a 20 KW xenon searchlight were all included to make finding the targets as easy as killing them.

While the AC-47s had carried only a six-man crew, Spectre carried twelve. Along with the pilot, copilot and navigator carried by any Herky Bird, Spectre had a fire control officer (FCO), three sensor operators, a crew chief and four gunner/loaders.

Initially three C-130s were converted to Spectre gunships. Two were still at Eglin Air Force Base in Florida, undergoing testing of even more advanced weapons and sensor systems. The third was doing live fire testing over Laos. If the prototype Spectre proved to be as effective in action as its designers hoped, it would soon be followed by many more, fulfilling the long-standing ambition to shut down the supply route to a trickle.

A SOLITARY Russian-built MiG-21PF jet fighter, code-named Fishbed D in the NATO nomenclature system, cruised over Laos's Steel Tiger area. Unlike the bare-metal-finished MiGs that rose from the NVAF airfields in North Vietnam to contest the airspace over their homeland, this particular fighter had been camouflaged. Atop a dull coat of medium green a leopard spot mottle of darker green had been applied in an irregular pattern to break up the outline of the sleek fighter. The yellow-star-and-bar national markings of the NVAF on the wings and aft fuselage were small and impossible to identify from more than a hundred meters even in daylight.

In the MiG's cockpit North Vietnamese air force Major Nguyen Van Tuy patiently searched the sky in front of him. The mobile Ground Control Intercept (GCI) radar station that had been specially set up for this mission had vectored him to this sector of south-eastern Laos.

"Green Dragon, this is Victory Control," the radar operator reported. "The target is circling at an altitude of eighteen hundred meters on a bearing of 260."

"This is Green Dragon," Tuy answered. "Understand eighteen hundred meters, bearing 260."

The pilot flicked the switch to the R1L gun-laying radar and the screen came alive, the green glow showing the blip at a range of five kilometers ahead of him and eight hundred meters below. He banked his fighter to the right, and there it was! Outlined against the moonlit sky was the unmistakable shape of a four-engine Lockheed C-130.

Now that he had visual contact on the Yankee air pirate he flicked off the radar and activated his gunsight. Dropping the speed of his ship to match the Spectre, Tuy maneuvered slightly above and directly behind the Yankee gunship. So far there was no sign that the Americans were aware of his presence. The Russian GRU reports stated that the Spectre wasn't equipped with air threat warning radar, and it seemed that Military Intelligence was correct for a change. All too often in the past the money they spent for information about American aircraft was outdated by the time the North Vietnamese air force received it.

He selected "guns" on his weapons control panel, flipped the safety cover up on his control stick and curled his finger around the trigger to the GP-9 twin-barrel GSh-23 cannon pack fitted to the belly of the MiG. Had Tuy simply intended to destroy the Spectre he would have been armed with the K-13 air-to-air heat-seeking missile or the K-13A radar-guided variant. A single hit from the missile's thirteen-pound warhead in the right place would have sent the gunship plummeting.

His mission tonight, however, wasn't simply to destroy the Spectre, but to force it down. Therefore, his ship had been armed with the cannon pack. To prevent the Spectre from catching fire, the cannon's magazines were feeding straight armor-piercing rounds to the guns, not the usual mix of AP and HE. He had two hundred rounds in the magazines for the fast-firing 23 mm cannons, more than enough to do the job.

Centering the gun sight's lighted pip on the Spectre's outer starboard engine nacelle, he tightened his finger on the trigger and the cannon pack spouted flame.

Since the MiG was firing straight AP loads, Tuy didn't have the flashes from the detonation of high-explosive warheads to tell him that he was on target, but the tracers in the base of the AP shells converged on the turboprop. The three-bladed prop quickly came to a stop, hanging motionless in the air.

The Spectre suddenly straightened out of its turn and started evasive action. Tuy smiled behind his helmet visor as he bore in even closer, easily following the big plane as it tried to escape. Centering the lighted pip of his gun sight in the outer turboprop on the other side of the plane, he touched the trigger lightly and sent a dozen 23 mm rounds smashing into the turboprop engine and it, too, died.

A small flame appeared at the rear of the nacelle, but it quickly died out as the American pilot hit the fire extinguisher for that engine. Tuy smiled; his mission would be a failure if the Spectre burned.

With two engines out the Spectre's pilot stopped throwing the aircraft around the sky and dropped its nose, trying to gain enough speed to make a run for it.

Tuy had been well briefed on the American plane's capabilities and knew that the other two four-thousand-horsepower turboprops were enough to keep the big ship in the air. One more engine had to be knocked out.

As Tuy closed in on the stricken ship, the rear ramp door suddenly opened and he saw the backlit figures of the crew frantically dumping boxes. With only two engines functional they needed to lessen the weight of the ship in a hurry. Knowing that the gunship would crash-land more easily if it was lighter, Tuy backed off and let the crew lighten their ship.

When the last of the ammo boxes and loose equipment were thrown out, Tuy closed in again. By the light of the full moon he could see the Laotian plain below and the foothills of the mountains. It was time to put an end to this Yankee air pirate while he was still over flat ground and could make a landing.

Slowly advancing his throttle, he closed the gap between the two planes until the Spectre's number two turboprop filled his gun sight. A light touch on the trigger sent half a dozen 23 mm armor-piercing cannon shells into the turbine and it seized up, bringing the propeller to an abrupt halt.

With three engines out the Spectre quickly headed for the ground. In the cockpit of the stricken AC-130 the pilot fought to bring his crippled plane in for a landing. If the MiG had left him two engines, it would have been a piece of cake. Hell, he could have flown all the way back to his home base in Thailand with two engines running. But with only one of the four-thousand-horsepower turboprops still turning, the Spectre had assumed the glide angle of a brick. The only good thing about his situation was that the MiG's cannon fire had pierced the gunship's self-sealing fuel tanks, and they were quickly draining dry. That greatly reduced the chance of fire when the plane hit the ground.

Immediately below was an open area with no vegetation. Holding constant rudder and aileron pressure to compensate for having power on only one wing, the pilot dropped to final approach for the wheels-up landing. A mere hundred meters above the ground the last turboprop flamed out for lack of fuel. The pilot barely had time to hit the crash alarm button before the plane struck the ground.

With the plane's controls set for single-engine flight, the sudden loss of power snapped the port-side wing down and the wingtip dug into the ground. The plane started to cartwheel, pivoting on the left wing, but the strain was too much for the damaged main wing spar, which snapped, folding the wing back against the fuselage and causing the plane to right itself.

The wing, however, had dragged the fuselage off the pilot's planned landing path, twisting it to the left. With a cry of alarm the pilot covered his face as the plane's nose drove into a rise in the ground at over one hundred miles per hour. The front of the plane crushed, the fuselage bounced back up into the air, skidded another two hundred meters and finally came to a stop, lying half on its side.

For a long moment nothing moved in the plane. But when the stunned crewmen heard the whine of the MiG's jet engine overhead, they fled the wreckage.

Tuy dived for the crash site, his finger curled around the trigger of his cannon pack. In the silvery moonlight he saw the small figures race for cover. Centering them in the glowing pip of his gun sight, he triggered the cannons again. The glowing tracers disappeared into the shadowed terrain, and he saw the figures fall to the ground.

The pilot racked his MiG around in a low turn and made another strafing run on the fleeing Americans. When he pulled out of his dive this time, he saw no further movement on the ground.

Circling above the crash, Tuy keyed his helmet microphone. "Victory Control, this is Green Dragon," he radioed to the mobile GCI operator. "The chicken has laid an egg in sector four. I repeat, the chicken has laid an egg in sector four. Over."

"This is Victory Control," the GCI station came back. "I understand the egg is in sector four."

Tuy dropped low to the ground and, flicking his cannon pack control switch to safe, set a course back to North Vietnam. A quick glance at his fuel gauges showed him that he should be able to make the auxiliary airfield at Tron Noi with several gallons to spare. A faint smile crossed his face when he thought about adding another red star kill marking on the front of his MiG in the morning. This was his fourth kill. He needed only one more before he would be an ace.

2

Northern Laos

At the far north end of the Laotian plain Soviet Major Yuri Yermolav of the GRU, the Russian Military Intelligence, Technical Intelligence Section, listened intently as Green Dragon radioed that the Spectre was down. So far the operation was going exactly as planned. The American gunship was on the ground and it hadn't burned on impact. The only real risk in this bold plan to capture the gunship had been that the plane would be destroyed in the crash. The extensive training Green Dragon had undergone in preparation for this mission had paid off.

The MiG pilot chosen for the mission was considered the best aerial gunner in the North Vietnamese air force. To further hone his gunnery skills, Tuy had practiced shooting at full-size mock-ups of American C-130 Hercules transport planes until every round fired had hit the target area—the plane's engines. When he was scoring perfectly on the mock-ups, he had been sent up for a graduation exercise against a live target. A Russian-made Ilyushin Il-18 four-engine transport plane, roughly the same size as a Hercules, had been chosen as his intended kill.

The Ilyushin had been piloted by a North Vietnamese air force volunteer who had tried to evade Tuy's MiG fighter and present as difficult a target as possible. But just as with the Spectre, Green Dragon had shot out the Ilyushin's engines one after the other until the plane had fallen out of the sky.

It was unfortunate that the target's pilot hadn't made it out of the plane before it had crashed. But, as Ho Chi Minh was fond of saying, "Victory will not come without great sacrifice from the people."

Yermolav switched off the radio and turned to the North Vietnamese army lieutenant standing beside him. "Thieu Uy Vinh, have the ground troops move in to secure the site. The helicopter with the recovery team will take off at first light."

Lieutenant Vinh saluted. "Yes, sir."

Yermolav checked his watch and glanced eastward. The sun would rise in a couple of hours, and by noon he would have all the fire control equipment out of the wreck and be taking it back to Hanoi en route to Rodina, Mother Russia. And, as far as Yermolav was concerned, it wouldn't be a minute too soon.

The stocky blond Russian had enjoyed just about all of Southeast Asia that he could stand. Living in Hanoi for the two months it had taken to put this operation together had been bad enough. The past week he had spent in this remote northern Laotian village waiting for the operation to start had been more than any civilized man should have to endure.

His ordeal was almost over. In a few hours the stifling heat, the inedible food and the ever-present swarms of insects would be behind him and he would be on his way back to Russia. His stomach rumbled, and he reached for the small pile of torn newsprint lying on the edge of the radio table. Clutching a handful of the paper, he ran for the latrine behind the hut.

IN THE WRECK of the Spectre Major "Nails" Hammer awoke to the overwhelming smell of JP-4. He was still strapped to his seat, but in the crash the seat had torn from its mountings and had slammed against the bulkhead. The Spectre's fuselage was tilted slightly to the right, and the groggy Hammer had to right his seat before he could unbuckle his seat harness.

As soon as he realized where he was, Hammer scrambled out of his harness. His first impulse was to help his crewmates escape before the wreckage caught fire, but halfway up to the forward door he paused at the steps leading to the flight deck. In the dim red glow of the interior lighting he saw there was no point in going up there to look for survivors. From where he stood he could see that both Rhodes and his copilot were dead. The cockpit had been crushed and the canopy framing had been driven into their bodies. Blood, looking glossy black in the red light, had pooled on the metal floor plates under their feet.

He noticed that the plane's navigator wasn't at his station and, glancing back through the plane's fuselage, he saw that the entire ship was empty. Apparently the rest of the crew had abandoned ship right after impact.

As he stepped from the open door of the plane, he saw the bodies of the crew lying scattered on the ground several meters away. It looked as if they had been gunned down. A quick check showed that the crewmen were all dead, their bodies torn to shreds by heavy-caliber fire. Apparently the MiG that had shot them down had made a strafing run after the crash.

As he counted the bodies, he realized that two men were missing: the crew chief, Master Sergeant Rusty Kegan, and one of the loaders, a new kid whose name he didn't remember. Pulling the .38-caliber revolver from his shoulder holster, he prowled around the rear of the wreck. There was no one by the plane's tail, so he started over to check a clump of bush a few meters away.

"Major Hammer," came a whisper from the bush in front of him, "is that you?"

Hammer dropped into a crouch, the .38 leveled at the bushes. "Who is it?"

"Sergeant Kegan, sir. I'm coming out."

The crew chief crawled out from his cover. "Jesus, sir, am I ever glad to see you. We thought you'd been killed in the crash."

Hammer rubbed the back of his head. "No," he said, ignoring the throbbing headache he suddenly realized he had. "I'm okay. How about you?"

"I'm fine, sir," Kegan responded, "but Jonesy's in pretty bad shape. He took a round in the leg and it really tore up his thigh."

"Where is he?"

Kegan pointed back into the bush. "I carried him back there and put a bandage on his leg. He passed out with the pain, but maybe that's best."

"Did you get the first-aid bag out of the plane?"

Kegan shook his head. "No, sir. When the MiG hit Jones, I just grabbed him and ran."

"Let's get the aid bag. It'll have morphine in it."

The first-aid bag was hanging on its hooks by the rear ramp door. Hammer retrieved it and handed it to Kegan. "Give Jones a shot of morphine. I'm going back in to see what else I can find."

Back inside the Spectre Hammer searched for weapons, but the M-16 rifles they normally carried in case they were forced down had been thrown out when the crew tried to lighten the ship. "Oh, fuck," he muttered when he realized what had happened to the rifles.

He still had his .38-caliber pistol, but he would have felt more comfortable with something that could reach out a little farther. Finding a full canteen that had been overlooked, he clipped it onto the belt of his flight suit. He also found one of the survival vests and shrugged it on. The small RT-10 survival radio in the vest pocket was going to be their ticket home.

When he stepped outside, he could see the faint outlines of the foothills in the moonlight to the southeast. The RT-10 survival radio was powerful, but he needed to be as high as possible for the signal to reach Hillsboro, the high-flying C-130 airborne command post and radio relay station on duty over the border region twenty-four hours a day.

Back in the bush Kegan gave Jones some morphine and tried to make the wounded man comfortable. "Chief," Hammer said, pointing to the hills, "I found a survival radio and I'm going to climb as high as I can to try to get through to Hillsboro control. You hold tight here with him."

Kegan's eyes darted around the shadows. "Yes, sir."

About half an hour later Hammer reached the top of the nearest hill. He was drenched in sweat and breathing hard from the run and the climb. Without pause he took the RT-10 radio from his flight suit pocket and switched it on.

"Hillsboro, Hillsboro," he radioed. "This is Spectre Two Eight Three on Guard channel. Does anyone read Spectre Two Eight Three?"

"Spectre Two Eight Three," came the tinny voice from the radio's small speaker. "This is Hillsboro. I read you weak but steady. Who am I talking to?"

"Major Norman Hammer, the FCO."

"Roger, Spectre. Wait one. Out."

There was a pause while Hillsboro called back to the Spectre's home base in Thailand to get the information from the personal data sheet Hammer had filled out before the flight. Since the aircrew didn't carry radio code books with them to authenticate their transmissions, correct answers to these personal questions would prove that Hillsboro was talking to a downed American flyer and not an English-speaking North Vietnamese.

"Spectre, what's your wife's maiden name?" Hillsboro radioed.

"My ex-wife's maiden name is Williams," Hammer radioed back. "My first car was a pink Rambler Rebel and I don't have a dog."

"Roger, you are now Spectre Alpha," Hillsboro said, confirming the answers to the personal data. "What is the status of the other Spectres?"

"Two of them are still alive. Sergeant Kegan, the crew chief, isn't hurt, but one of the gunners is wounded. We need an SAR with a medic in here ASAP, over."

"Roger, we're scrambling Sandy SAR from NKP right now. Is there any sign of enemy activity in your vicinity?"

"That's a negative right now," Hammer answered. "Everything's quiet."

"That's good," Hillsboro answered. "Gather up your remaining chicks and find a good place to hole up until Sandy Flight gets on-station. I'll give you a call when they're ten minutes out."

"Roger, Hillsboro. We'll be waiting. Spectre Alpha out."

Hammer switched the survival radio over to listen only and stuffed it back into the leg pocket of his flight suit as he started back down the rocky hill.

INSIDE THE CAMBODIAN border several hundred miles to the south, American Special Forces Captain Mike Reese lay motionless in a clump of bush halfway down a ridge line, his field glasses held up to his eyes. In the valley a few meters below him a North Vietnamese infantry battalion was breaking camp and preparing to move out. It was still dark, but with the light of the full moon Reese's field glasses gave him a clear view of what was going on.

Spread out in the bush on both sides of him were five other Special Forces men. One of them was American, Sergeant First Class Victor Hotchkiss. The other members of the recon patrol were Nungs, the ethnic Chinese tribesmen who flocked to enlist in the Special Forces units so that they could fight the hated Communists.

All six men were dressed in the black, green and tan-striped camouflage uniforms known as "tiger suits." Green and black camouflage paint covered their exposed skin, and they wore tiger stripe boonie hats. The Nungs were armed with M-16 rifles. Hotchkiss and Reese carried CAR-15s, the submachine gun versions of the 16.

Reese and his men were from Special Forces Company A-410, a Mike Force unit, or Mobile Strike Force, stationed in Dak Sang, a remote camp on the South Vietnamese-Cambodian border. A-410 wasn't merely one more Special Forces Mike Force company. It was a MACV-SOG Hatchet Force unit, a ready-reaction force to be used to back up the clandestine SOG Shining Brass recon teams that operated deep behind enemy lines in Laos, Cambodia and North Vietnam.

On Hatchet Force operations Reese's mission was to put platoon-size units across the border at a moment's notice to go to the assistance of an RT in trouble or to exploit a contact in the supposedly neutral countries bordering South Vietnam. This was a war that wasn't shown to the American public on the six o'clock news. In fact, MACV-SOG's secret war wasn't even known to most U.S. senior military officials, but it was a war nonetheless. And, for Reese and the men of Mike Force Company A-410, it was the only war they knew.

Because of the casualties they had taken in a determined NVA assault on their new border camp at the first of the month, A-410 wasn't up to strength to undertake these platoon-size operations yet. SOG, however, was always short of warm bodies for its clandestine war, so Reese's headquarters, Command and Control Central in Kontoum, was using A-410's manpower for smaller recon patrols across the border, like the one they were on now.

Reese's orders were to locate the NVA unit as it moved in from Cambodia and to track it when it crossed over into South Vietnamese territory so that a B-52 Arc Light strike could be called in on their heads. He had finally located his target, and as soon as the sun rose, his small team would dog the enemy's heels until the high-flying B-52s could fly over and bomb them into oblivion.

So far it had been a fairly routine mission. They had located the North Vietnamese easily enough, and they hadn't been spotted. If the rest of the mission went as planned, they would be calling for the Arc Light by tomorrow morning, do the BDA, the Bomb Damage Assessment, after the bombing run, and get the hell out.

"Moon Dog, Moon Dog," came the faint, tinny voice from the radio handset clipped to Reese's assault harness. "This is Black Snake, over."

Reese reached up and clicked the talk switch on the radio handset three times. Black Snake was the radio call sign for CCC, Command and Control Central, Reese's Special Forces headquarters back across the border in Kontoum, RVN. Clicking the microphone switch, breaking squelch as it was called, three times was a signal to the caller that Reese couldn't talk to him right now because he was too close to the enemy and might be overheard.

"Moon Dog, Moon Dog," the radio operator said urgently. "This is a Blue Star call. Over."

Reese snatched the radio handset and held it up to his ear. Blue Star messages had the highest priority and required immediate attention. "This is Moon Dog One One," he whispered. "Go ahead."

"This is Black Snake. Message from Snake Three. 'Surf's Up.' I say again, 'Surf's Up.' How copy? Over."

Reese paused for a moment. "Surf's Up" was the monthly code word to break off the mission and run for home. He glanced down at his watch and saw that it was 0548. What in hell was going on this early in the morning? "Moon Dog One One," he radioed. "Copy 'Surf's Up,' over."

"This is Black Snake. Proceed to Lima Zulu Delta for immediate extraction, over."

"One One," Reese answered. "Roger Lima Zulu Delta. My Echo Tango Alpha is six zero, out."

Clipping the handset back on his harness, Reese motioned for the team to pull out. In the light of the full moon he saw the looks of surprise on the faces of his SF team members, so he pumped his arm, indicating that they should move out fast. One by one the team members pulled out of their observation point and faded back into the bush.

It took almost half an hour for the team to get back behind the ridge line and safely out of sight from the NVA encampment in the valley. Once in the clear, they double-timed through the light bush to their prearranged pickup site a klick and a half away from the valley.

3

Nhakon Phanom, Thailand

The three planes roared down the concrete runway of the Royal Thai air force base, the thunder of their three twenty-eight-hundred-horsepower Wright radial piston engines echoing across the tarmac like the soundtrack from a World War II aviation movie. The planes creating this man-made thunder looked like something out of a World War II movie, as well. Their upper surfaces were painted in flat green and tan camouflage colors. Olive-drab high-explosive bombs and white rocket pods hung under their wings. All they lacked was the colorful pinups and personal names that had adorned the noses of their predecessors.

These flying antiques were known to the Air Force pilots who flew them as A-1H Super Spads, but once they had been known as the Douglas AD-1 Skyraider, the Navy's famous Korean War all-purpose attack bomber. Armed with four 20 mm cannons in the wings and able to carry a greater bomb load than a World War II B-17 Flying Fortress, the Super Spads could do what no modern jet fighter bomber could do: fly low and slow and drop their ordnance with great accuracy. Also, having been designed as Navy carrier aircraft, they had great range and could loiter in the sky for ten hours, waiting for a target to appear. Or, in this case, they could stay on-station to protect the rescue choppers when they tried to locate and extract the flyers from the downed Spectre.

It was 0613, and dawn was just breaking in the east when the Spads pulled up their landing gear and banked away to fly into the rising sun. By the time the Sandy Search and Rescue flight married up with the HH-53 Jolly Green Giant SAR chopper and reached the Spectre's crash site in Laos, it would be daylight.

IT WAS STILL DARK when Mike Reese stepped off the Huey Slick at the Kontoum helipad and saw that Major Jan Snow, CCC's operations officer, was waiting for him. "Sorry to snatch you out of the woods like that," the S-3 said quickly, "but we've just had a real problem dumped on us and I need your help."

Reese was taken aback at Snow's tone of voice and the worried look on his face. The Hungarian-born officer was known in Special Forces circles as "the Iceman," and if he was worried, then Reese surmised that something had gone completely tits up.

"What's going down, sir?"

"It seems the Air Force just lost one of its most secret aircraft over the Ho Chi Minh Trail in southeastern Laos. SOG wants us to go in and secure it for them until they can fly a salvage team in to recover the classified black boxes."

"What kind of plane is it?"

"An AC-130A Spectre."

"What in hell is that?" Reese frowned. "I've never heard of it."

"It's some kind of super Spooky gunship proto-type," Snow replied. "It's the only one in-country, and they're anxious that the classified gear it carries stays out of the hands of the Dinks."

"Why in hell did they lose it then?"

Snow let a faint smile tug at the corners of his mouth. "They say it was shot down by a MiG."

"Jesus," Reese said. "What was a MiG doing down there? I thought they never left their home turf."

"That's what the blue suiters want to know," Snow said dryly. "Come on inside and I'll fill you in."

Lieutenant Colonel Ron Newman, CCC's com-mander, was talking on the operations room phone when Reese and Snow walked in. He glanced up, his face grim, and motioned for Reese to help himself from the coffeepot on the filing cabinet. A map of Laos was laid out on the table. Reese walked over to it. A big red circle had been drawn around a plain in the area of southeastern Laos known as Steel Tiger.

"Sorry to call you back in the middle of an opera-tion, Reese," Newman said, putting the phone down in its cradle. "But MACV's really jumping through their ass on this one, and even the Joint Chiefs have gotten in on the action. We've been ordered in no un-certain terms to get the classified equipment out of that crashed plane at all costs."

Reese didn't like the sound of those orders at all, but he knew better than to argue about it. Every man in a Special Forces SOG unit was a triple volunteer: he had volunteered for Airborne training, he had volunteered for Special Forces and he had volunteered for SOG duty in-country. "Where do we come in, sir?"

"It's your turn in the barrel," Newman said. "I have to put a team in there ASAP, and your people are available."

"How many people do they want?" Reese asked. "And when do we go?"

"I want you to take your XO and five other men," Newman said, raising his hand to forestall Reese's objection to his ordering both of the A-team's officers on the same dangerous mission. "Your team sergeant can run the camp until you get back. Because of the classified equipment involved," Newman went on to explain, "MACV wants to have at least two officers on the mission." He paused. "For the same reason you can take only one of your Nungs with you."

"But, sir, they're asking me to send half of the SF on my team," Reese protested. Normally on a mission of that size only two of the A-team's Americans would go and the rest would be Nungs. That way, if something went wrong, the A-team wouldn't be destroyed. "And, as you know, sir, I'm already one man short. My heavy weapons specialist, Sergeant Rohm, was Medevaced to Japan, and I haven't gotten a replacement for him yet."

"I know," Newman said, "but those are my orders. That's how hot this thing is."

"Yes, sir," Reese said, accepting the inevitable. "When do we move out and what are we supposed to do when we get there?"

Newman walked over to the map. "They still haven't sent us an exact fix on the crash site. But their last radio transmission was from this general area." His finger tapped the southern end of the circled plain. "MACV's ordered a Blackbird aerial recon of the area, and the photos will be flown here as soon as they come in. Once we have them we'll have a better idea of what you're going to be up against over there.

"Until then," Newman continued, "I want you to go back to Dak Sang, brief your people, get your gear together and get back here as fast as you can. By then we should know where the crash is. There's a Slick waiting outside to take you back to your camp."

Reese drained the last of the coffee in his cup. "On the way, sir."

MAJOR "NAILS" HAMMER had reached level ground again as dawn broke over the Laotian plains. He was starting back to the wreck when he heard the unmistakable sound of helicopter rotors approaching in the distance. He frowned; Sandy wasn't due to show up for another half hour or so. Reaching into his pant pocket, he brought out his survival radio and switched it on.

"Hillsboro," he radioed, "this is Spectre Alpha."

"Hillsboro, go ahead."

"Do you have Sandy Flight in the area yet?"

"Their ETA is still two zero. Why?"

"I hear what sounds like a chopper approaching from the north."

"I'm afraid it's not one of ours, Spectre," Hillsboro answered tensely. "You'd better find a place to hide."

"You've got that shit right. Spectre out."

Hammer stuffed the radio back into his pocket and raced for the wreck to warn Sergeant Kegan and Jones about the enemy aircraft. Since Kegan didn't have a radio, he wouldn't know the approaching chopper wasn't the Sandy rescue flight.

As he approached the plane, he saw figures walking around it. He wasn't close enough yet to see details of their uniforms, but he slowed his headlong run to a jog and kept close to the scattered clumps of bush. He was about two hundred and fifty meters from the wreck when someone suddenly stepped out of the vegetation a few meters in front of him—a North Vietnamese soldier in a dark olive uniform and a pith helmet, carrying an AK-47 assault rifle.

Though the NVA's back was to him, Hammer threw himself behind a nearby rock in a panic. As he landed, he felt his thigh slam into a projection on the rock and heard a sickening crunch. He didn't have to look to know he had crushed the small radio. Now what in hell was he going to do?

Soviet Major Yuri Yermolav stepped off the Soviet-built North Vietnamese Mi-4 helicopter and looked at the wrecked Spectre. Even as crumpled wreckage it was a beautiful airplane. Only the Americans could have thought of something as ingenious as mounting automatic weapons to fire out the side of a transport plane and using it as a ground-attack gunship. With the capture of the American fire control and sensor systems, however, it wouldn't be too long before the Soviet air force would have such a potent machine in their aerial inventory, as well.

As a technical intelligence officer specializing in aircraft, Yermolav was very much aware of the importance of capturing the latest examples of American aviation technology for examination in the Soviet Union. He knew all too well that if it wasn't for the advanced Western technology taken from captured and stolen equipment, the Soviet air force would probably still be flying propeller-driven aircraft.

The first primitive Soviet jets had been powered by World War II German engines. But ever since the British had so foolishly sold the Soviets the advanced Rolls-Royce Nene jet engine in 1947, most of the significant advances in Soviet aircraft design had come from the West. Even the K-13 air-to-air missiles carried by the MiG jet fighters were copies of the American Sidewinder missiles.

Lieutenant Vinh spoke briefly with the NVA infantry sergeant in charge of the security element that had arrived to secure the site before the chopper had landed.

"Comrade Major," Vinh said, "the sergeant has informed me that he has captured two of the Yankee air pirates. The rest of the crew was killed in the attack."

"Take me to them."

The North Vietnamese sergeant led Yermolav to a small clearing in the bush where two Americans in olive-drab flight suits were guarded by several Vietnamese riflemen. The oldest of the captives wore the stripes of a master sergeant. The wounded younger man's uniform was bare of insignia, but he had to be one of the crew. He didn't have the look of an officer.

"See to that man's wound," Yermolav said, pointing at Jones. "And rig a litter for him. We'll be taking them with us when we go."

The Yankee sergeant's eyes followed him as he spoke, but Yermolav ignored him. He had more important things on his mind right now. The interrogation would come later when he got the captives back to Hanoi.

Inside the wreck Yermolav was examining the low-light television set at one of the sensor stations, when one of the Vietnamese infantrymen came running up the rear ramp. Lieutenant Vinh spun around. "Comrade Major!" he said. "The sergeant reports that a Yankee rescue flight is approaching!"

Yermolav raced back outside, brushing Vinh aside. To the east he saw two dark specks approaching in the sky. He glanced over at the Mi-4 that had transported him and his salvage team to the crash site, then back up at the rapidly approaching American planes. Whatever they were, they were coming on fast, much too fast.

"Take off!" Yermolav shouted at the helicopter pilot, waving his arms.

The North Vietnamese pilot didn't speak Russian, but it was obvious what the Soviet wanted. He hit the starter button for the big radial piston engine in the nose of the Mi-4. As Yermolav turned to run back into the bush to hide, the helicopter's engine started with a puff of gray smoke and the rotors started to turn.

AIR FORCE CAPTAIN Slick Dodson, the pilot of Sandy One and the flight leader for the rescue mission, looked down at the Laotian plain known as Steel Tiger. The three A-1H Super Spads were at five thousand feet and maximum throttle, giving them an airspeed of well over three hundred miles an hour. Sandy Control back at Nhakon Phanom had told him to get on-site as fast as he could, and the Spad pilots were doing exactly that. The Jolly Green Giant rescue chopper was still several minutes behind, because even at top speed it couldn't keep up with the powerful attack planes.

Dodson keyed his throat mike. "All Sandies, this is Sandy One. We're coming up on it. Keep a sharp eye out. Hillsboro says our man on the ground has reported hearing enemy aircraft, maybe a chopper."

Below him the foothills flattened out into the scrub-brush-covered plain, and from his height Sandy One immediately spotted the scrape in the red earth made by the Spectre's crash landing. "There it is," he radioed. "Two o'clock at about three klicks. It landed in that brushy area about a kick from the hills."

As Sandy One closed in on the crash site, he spotted the olive-green shape of a single-rotor helicopter sitting on the ground behind the wreck. It looked a little like one of the old Sikorsky S-55 helicopters that had seen wide use in the Army and Air Force as the H-19. The pilot paused for a second, remembering that the South Vietnamese air force also used a few of them, then he saw the yellow-star-and-bar insignia on the side of the ship. It was a Russian-built North Vietnamese Mi-4 helicopter, and the main rotor was turning!

Sandy One charged his guns and switched on his gun sight as he nosed his Spad down for a firing run on the enemy ship as it lifted off. Since he had the enemy chopper cold, he didn't bother to pickle the ordnance he carried under his wings. All it would take was one run to splash this guy, and he might need the bombs later.

So rarely did an American fighter pilot ever get a chance to fire on a North Vietnamese aircraft that Sandy One didn't stop to think why it was at the Spectre crash site. All he could think of was painting a red star kill marking on the cowling of his Spad.

Centering the enemy aircraft in the middle of his lighted pip, Sandy One's finger tightened on the gun trigger. The Super Spad's four wing-mounted 20 mm cannons hammered, and he watched his tracers disappear into the center of the Mi-4's olive green fuselage.

The chopper staggered in the air under the blows of the cannons. Sparkles of fire appeared where the 20 mm high-explosive rounds exploded on contact with the helicopter's thin aluminum skin. The 20 mm armor-piercing rounds, however, smashed through the airframe, tearing into the high-octane fuel tanks.

With light movements on the controls Sandy One shifted his point of aim forward and sent a long burst of 20 mm shells into the chopper's large cockpit area. The canopy shattered and pieces of Plexiglas flew outward. With dead hands on the controls the Mi-4 plummeted to earth.

Twenty feet off the ground the chopper exploded in a ball of flame. The rotor blades spun off, and the blazing wreckage smashed to earth several hundred meters from the Spectre.

Pulling out of his dive, Sandy One flashed over the burning wreckage. The pilot had to fight the urge to throw his fighter into a victory roll over the burning wreckage; the bombs hanging under his wings prevented any acrobatics.

"Yippee!" the pilot shouted over the radio as he hauled back on his control stick to climb into the sky again. "I got 'em. I got the motherfucker!"

While his two wingmen circled above, Sandy One banked in a low orbit over the Spectre. "I can't see anyone down there," he called up to the orbiting Jolly Green. "And I'm not getting any radio signals. Whoever was on that chopper must have policed our guys up."

He didn't bother to add that his shooting down the enemy helicopter had probably killed any American survivors from the Spectre.

4

Dak Sang Mike Force Camp, RVN

The sun was just coming up over the jungle-covered hills of the Dak Sang Valley when Reese stepped off the slick back at his camp. Having been alerted by the returning members of the aborted recon patrol, Master Sergeant Ray Pierce, his team sergeant, and First Lieutenant Jack Santelli, his executive officer, were waiting for him at the helipad.

"What's the word, *Dai Uy?*" Santelli asked, following the Special Forces custom of using the Vietnamese word for Reese's rank.

Reese studied his XO for a moment. The slim, dark-haired officer was almost hopping from one foot to the other, waiting to hear that they had orders to go out in the woods and kill more enemy soldiers. In the past two and a half weeks since the NVA assault on the camp had been beaten back, Santelli had been busy day and night rebuilding the damage and tending to the thousand and one administrative details that made up the daily life of a military unit's executive officer. Santelli was a good XO, but he was an even better combat leader. After the inactivity of the past several days, he was chomping at the bit to get back into the field.

"You're going to love this one, Jack," Reese said, grinning broadly. "How'd you like to take a little trip to southern Laos?"

Santelli's grin threatened to split his face. "Outfuckingstanding! That's the best news I've heard in weeks, Captain. When do we leave?"

Reese laughed. "ASAP. Get the guys together in the bunker and I'll go over it."

It was only a few minutes before all of the A-team were assembled in the camp's command bunker. Like Santelli, most of the men were bored with sitting around the camp and were willing to do just about anything that promised to break the monotony—even going to war.

"Okay," Reese said, "here's the story. The Air Force lost a plane in the Steel Tiger area of Laos earlier this morning." He pointed to the map. "This thing's a prototype gunship, some kind of Super Spooky, and it's loaded with highly classified fire control and sensor gear. MACV wants us to go in, secure the crash site and help the blue suiters recover their lost goodies."

A wide, boyish grin split Santelli's face. As far as he was concerned, this sounded great. But Sergeant Pierce, who was standing next to him, didn't share his youthful enthusiasm.

Master Sergeant Ray Pierce had been in the Army since he had enlisted at the age of seventeen to go to the Korean War; he had seen more combat in the eighteen years since then to last any man a lifetime or two. His dark reddish hair and bronze skin marked his

Santee Sioux ancestry on his mother's side and the Irish of his father's. Having been raised on a ranch in Montana by his mother's people, he had been steeped in the warrior's tradition long before he'd ever put on his first set of Army fatigues. Eighteen years of infantry and Special Forces duty all over the world had only honed that earlier training to a razor's edge.

On his third tour of duty in Southeast Asia with the Special Forces, Pierce was a canny old warrior whose primary philosophy of life was to do it unto others before they did it unto him. He never backed away from a fight, but he liked to choose where and when he did unto others. That way he cut the risk that they would do unto him first.

This mission in Laos, however, could only spell trouble, and trouble far away from home. Working across the fence always had its risks, but working in Laos was far riskier than operating in Cambodia because it was farther away from support if anything went wrong.

"Now," Reese continued, "because of the nature of this operation, and the sensitive gear we're going after, MACV wants this to be an all round-eye show. We can only take one Nung interpreter with us."

That comment got surprised looks from everyone. The Nung troops who made up A-410's Mike Force company were the most dedicated anti-Communist fighters in all Southeast Asia. In a war where it was all too often difficult to tell who was friend and who was foe regardless of the uniform they wore, the Nungs could always be counted on. Their loyalty was so highly regarded that most South Vietnamese politicians and high-ranking officers used Nungs for their bodyguards because their own people couldn't be trusted.

This was the first time that any of these Special Forces men had ever heard of Nungs being restricted from sensitive operations. When Reese offered no explanation as to why this stipulation had occurred, they knew it had come from MACV or even the Pentagon.

"I'll be taking the mission out," Reese went on. "And I'm taking you, Jack." He nodded to the XO, who grinned back. "Along with Kowalski, Hotchkiss, Torres, Wilson and one of the camp interpreters."

He looked around the room. "Do any of you have problems with that?"

No one spoke.

"We'll be launching sometime this morning, and I don't have a mission closure time yet. I want you to pack for three days just in case. Get your shit together as fast as you can and report to the helipad. That Slick sitting out there will take us to CCC for a final briefing, and we'll use that as our launch point. Any questions?"

There were none. Every man on the team knew what a free-wheeling, cross-border mission like this was all about. Everything would be up in the air from the moment they crossed into Laos, and there was no point in asking questions that no one had any answers to.

"Okay, then," Reese said, "let's hit it."

Sergeant Pierce waited until the others had left before approaching his CO. "I should be going out with you on this one, sir," he said as he watched Reese gather his maps. "Santelli's good, but he's still a little green, if you know what I mean. You need to have someone with a little more cross-border experience. Things could go tits up over there real quick, and if they do, you'll need the old Indian with you."

"I know, Sarge," Reese agreed. "But SOG specifically wants two officers to go on this one because of the classified equipment in that plane."

"You mean they want to make sure they have someone to hang if something gets all fucked up."

Reese smiled grimly. "You've got that shit right, Sarge, but that's the way it is. Also CCC wants to keep the camp operational while we're gone, and that'll be your job. It's heating up across the fence, and the Iceman wants to be able to use us if he has to."

"I'm not worried about keeping things going around here," Pierce said. "I'll just have old Vao kick ass and take names for me. But I am worried about half of the team going across the fence at the same time. I'm getting too old to break in a new replacement team."

Reese laughed and patted his team sergeant on the shoulder. "Don't worry, Sarge. SOG's promised us all the support we need."

"That's what I'm afraid of, sir. The last time they promised us something like that, we damn near got our asses overrun."

When Reese walked into his hootch to get some additional gear, he saw a letter lying on his bed. He didn't have to read the return address to know it was from his soon-to-be ex-wife, Judy; he could recognize her distinctive handwriting from across the room. Reese reached for it, then pulled his hand back, not sure if he really wanted to open it right now. Whatever she had to say, it would only be more bad news, and he didn't have time for that kind of stuff right now.

Opening up his wall locker, he scooped the letter up and tossed it onto the top shelf unopened. Right now he had to get ready to go to war, and there would be time enough to read it when he returned. If he didn't come back, then it wouldn't really matter what her latest bitch was about.

For what had to have been the tenth time since Reese had gotten back in-country two months ago, he reminded himself that he had to make a trip to SFOB in Nha Trang and see the Fifth Group JAG officer about filing for a divorce. He had been busy with A-410 almost from the first day he had started his second tour, but that was no excuse. If he'd had time to go to Saigon, meet another woman and get involved with her, he should have been able to find time to take care of that little chore. This situation between him and his wife had gone on more than long enough, and he vowed that as soon as he got back from this mission, he would make that long-overdue trip.

As he started preparing for the mission, he tried to put his wife out of his mind. But, as always, that wasn't easy. Judy had always had a way of getting under his skin. At first it had been exciting to be with her. She was strong-willed, wildly passionate and had a real zest for life. But those traits didn't mean she had made a good military wife.

At first the Army had been a lark for her, something new and different. Reese's first duty station had been with the Tenth Special Forces Group in Bad Tolz, Germany, and Judy had loved the excitement and newness of living in Europe. That wore off soon enough, however. Judy was quickly bored, and even Europe hadn't been able to hold her interest for long. She had been glad when he was transferred back to the States for additional training before going overseas on his first combat tour in Vietnam.

During his first tour in Nam, Judy had been a properly supportive military wife. Unknown to him, however, she had expected him to leave the Army when he came home from Vietnam and had even lined up a job for him with her father's California real estate business. When he refused even to consider getting out of the Army on his return, the battle began. When he went on to Fort Benning at the end of his leave, he had traveled alone. Judy had refused to leave California.

For a time he had tried to work out a compromise, but she refused to back down an inch. Tired of fighting her by mail, he had volunteered to return to Vietnam, where he knew he at least had some chance of winning. All that was left between them now was an endless war. Even if he was to back down now and give up the Army for her, he knew things would never be the same between them.

As happened sooner or later in all marital wars, the line of no return had been passed, and going back to the way things had been was impossible. All he faced with her now was more marital combat. To complicate things even more, he had met Laura Winthrop in Saigon. She was a UPI reporter who had come to Dak Sang to write about the Special Forces. In the process of her research she had ended up in Reese's bed.

This had been a revelation for Reese; it had been so long since he had been with a woman who wasn't at war with him that he had forgotten how nice it could be. Although his relationship with Laura was in its initial tentative state where anything could happen, at least he had a good chance to build something with her. There was no chance he would ever have anything with Judy again.

Throwing the last of his gear into his rucksack, Reese shut the locker on his wife's letter and headed for the chopper pad at double time. Screw her and the horse she rode in on. He had a war to fight.

AS SOON AS THE SOUND of the Sandy Flight's A-1 Spad engines faded, Major Yermolav stepped out of his hiding place in the bush and stared at the rapidly disappearing American planes. His broad, beefy face was a frozen mask and, had he been alone, he would have shaken his fists in anger at the Yankees. He knew that such a gesture would only make him look like a fool in front of these men. He had lost too much face with them already.

The Russian technical expert didn't speak Vietnamese, but he didn't have to. He knew when the little bastards were talking about him. His stomach still rumbled from eating the stuff that passed for food in the Laotian village, and each time he'd had to run for the primitive latrine he had heard them laughing behind his back.

Regardless of the vaunted internationalism of Leninism, Yermolav was a Russian first and a Communist second. There was no way he was ever going to view the Vietnamese as being anything other than second class. As far as he was concerned, it was a sad day when a Russian had to live with barbarians. He had endless sympathy for the Russian pilots living in Hanoi who were trying to train the little bastards to fly the MiG fighters. They were stationed there for months on end, but he could go back to Mother Russia as soon as he could get this damn Yankee equipment transported north.

He looked back at the blazing wreckage of the Mi-4 helicopter that was to have taken him and the Spectre's equipment back to Hanoi. That was out now until he could get another helicopter flown in from the North, and he had no way of knowing how long that would take. The operation had already been postponed once because of maintenance problems with the NVAF's aging Russian helicopter fleet.

There was no way to tell how long it would take the North Vietnamese to get another Mi-4 helicopter out of maintenance and back into the air. Until that happened, he couldn't sit here and wait; there was too great a risk of further aerial attack by the Americans. Not only did Yermolav fear for his own personal safety, but also he couldn't risk having the salvaged American fire control equipment destroyed.

"Vinh!" he shouted, and the Russian-speaking North Vietnamese lieutenant came running. Even though this particular Vietnamese spoke passable Russian, as far as Yermolav was concerned, he was still little more than a trained monkey.

"Yes, Comrade Major!"

"We have to get this equipment out of here now. Tell that sergeant of yours to rig some slings and get it ready to be carried out of here."

"Where do you want it taken, Comrade?"

Yermolav pointed north.

5

Kadena Air Force Base, Okinawa

Kadena Air Force Base, Okinawa, was the home base of the Ninth Strategic Reconnaissance Wing of the United States Air Force, and the main function of the Ninth SRW was the care and feeding of the greatest aircraft ever built—the Lockheed SR-71 Blackbird. Born as the YF-12A advanced interceptor, capable of flying at speeds in excess of mach three at the upper limits of the atmosphere, the radical aircraft soon had its function changed to that of high-altitude aerial reconnaissance. Today's recon mission would take the Blackbird over the Steel Tiger area of southeastern Laos.

The 103-foot-long all-black aircraft looked more like a spaceship from a science fiction movie than an airplane as it was towed out of its hangar. The Blackbird's long, cobralike nose, with the small two-man cockpit set well forward, flared back into deep delta wings with rounded tips. Midway between where the wingtips and the roots blended smoothly into the fuselage were two of the largest jet engines in the world—the mighty 32,500-pound thrust, J-58 turbo-ramjet engines that burned an exotic hydrocarbon fuel specially formulated for them. Two large, inwardly canted, slab-sided tail fins sat on top of the rear of the engine nacelles. Two similar fins were folded to the side under the nacelles and would fold into place once the plane was airborne.

Two men wearing NASA-type astronaut spacesuits climbed out of an air-conditioned van and up the ladder into the cockpit of the Blackbird and started preflight checks. Even with help from the ground crew the checklist read-off took over an hour. Finally, with bright flames shooting out of her afterburners, the big, dull-black spy plane thundered down the eight-thousand-foot runway.

At the four-thousand-foot mark her nose gear rotated off the runway, and the Blackbird was airborne just as dawn broke over the island. As soon as the landing gear retracted, the pilot shoved his throttles forward even farther, and the big ship shot forward. In seconds it was climbing at over mach two to meet its tanker.

At twenty-five thousand feet over the Pacific Ocean the SR-71 made its rendezvous with the Boeing KC-135Q aerial tanker aircraft to refuel. The Blackbird's two huge J-58 engines were thirsty. She needed a long drink of JP-7 jet fuel before starting her high-speed recon run. Once refueled, the pilot of the SR-71 lit up the burners again. The spy plane quickly broke mach unity and streaked to her cruising altitude of eighty-five thousand feet, sixteen miles high in the sky.

Once at altitude, the Blackbird settled down to a cruising speed of mach 3.5, three and a half times the speed of sound, or two thousand miles per hour, as she turned north, heading for the landmass of Southeast Asia. The heat of her speed made the titanium skin on the aircraft's nose and the leading edge of her delta wings glow a dull orange-red at twelve hundred degrees Fahrenheit as she started her camera run along the border region shared by Cambodia, Laos and Vietnam.

In the back seat of the Blackbird the RSO, the recon systems operator, turned on his battery of cameras and sensors that could cover a path sixty miles wide along the aircraft's route. From eighty-five thousand feet the sensors he controlled could detect a burning cigarette at night and the cameras could read a newspaper's headlines.

Sixteen miles below the speeding SR-71 Major Yermolav's salvage team was operating, unaware of the spy plane's passage. But, even had the Russian technical officer known of the Blackbird's presence, there was absolutely nothing he or his North Vietnamese air force allies could have done about it. She was simply flying too fast and too high.

Several minutes later the SR-71 started turning slowly over southern Red China to head southeast again. It was a leisurely turn that took hundreds of miles to complete at the Blackbird's speed of mach 3.5, but the pilot wasn't at all concerned about being in Red Chinese airspace. There wasn't a fighter plane in the world that could reach him where he was, flying on the edge of space. Not even the most advanced Russian antiaircraft missiles could reach that high. At eighty-five thousand feet the sky was his own to do with as he pleased.

Once he had turned around, the pilot aimed his spy plane on a path that would take her over the Red Chinese border with North Vietnam, then south to Hanoi and Haiphong. He figured that as long as they were in the neighborhood, so to speak, he might as well use up the rest of the camera's film. He would just slip on down and take a look at what the French and Russian cargo ships were off-loading in Haiphong harbor.

A little over an hour later the SR-71 settled back down on the concrete runway at Kadena Air Force Base. Braking parachutes popped from the rear of the plane, and another Blackbird mission was completed. Soon the Blackbird's photos and sensor readouts were on their way to CCC at Kontoum, being delivered by an F-4 Phantom courier flight.

BY THE TIME Reese and his team arrived at CCC, the Blackbird's photos were waiting for them as well as a slight change in mission. Because of the risk involved in flying in a team of Air Force technicians to work at a crash site that far behind enemy lines, MACV wanted Reese's men to recover the classified equipment from the Spectre and evacuate it by Sky Hook.

While Lieutenant Santelli and the team went to double-check their weapons, ammunition and equipment, Reese followed Major Snow into the operations room. "I am sorry about the mission change," Snow said. "But now that we think there has been enemy activity in the vicinity of the wreckage, the Air

Force brass have changed their minds about sending their people in. They say their technicians are not trained to operate under those conditions."

Reese couldn't argue with that, and he knew it wasn't an indication of a lack of guts on the part of the blue suiters. Some of the bravest men he knew were the Air Force paramedics who rode the Jolly Green SAR flights when they went after downed American airmen in enemy territory.

"They have sent photos of the items they want you to recover," Snow said. He indicated a small canvas bag lying on the table. "Along with a tool kit for removing them and step-by-step instructions. Then, when they have been Sky-Hooked out and you are ready to extract, they want you to burn the wreck."

"The last part's no problem, sir," Reese said. "And I'll put Torres in charge of taking the stuff out. He's my radioman and he's good with electronics."

"Okay," Snow said, turning to a table covered with eight-by-eleven glossy photographs. "Now let's take a look at those recon photos."

Reese studied the SR-71 photos carefully, amazed to see the detail it was possible to get from sixteen miles up. The crashed AC-130 showed up clearly, as did the burned-out wreckage of what he was told had been a Russian Mi-4 helicopter with North Vietnamese markings. He saw the figures on the ground that had been identified as the bodies of the dead Spectre aircrew, but didn't see anyone who could be North Vietnamese or Pathet Lao troops.

"Where are the bad guys?" he asked.

"We think they were all in that chopper," Snow said. "The Sandy pilots didn't report seeing anyone after they splashed that bird, and the photo interpretation people didn't find anyone in the area."

Taking a handful of the photos over to the large-scale map of Laos, Reese compared the map to the photos. "If we put down here," he said, pointing to a clearing in the brush a few klicks from the downed Spectre, "we should be able to reach the crash site in under an hour. I don't want to land any closer than that in case someone's keeping an eye on it.

"I figure it'll take us an hour to move from the LZ to the crash site." Reese tapped the map. "And you said the Air Force tech people estimated an hour and a half to take out the gear, but let's call it two just to be on the safe side. And then it will take us half an hour more to rig the Sky Hooks to the package. That's three and a half hours on the ground, so let's add a fuck-up factor and call it four." He turned to face the Iceman. "Can the Air Force cover us for those four hours? We can't do any of this without air support we can count on."

"They will cover you for as long as it takes," Snow answered. "They plan to have a FAC, the Jolly Green, a flight of four Spads and an aerial tanker on-station throughout the operation. A flight of Fox Fours will also be on ramp alert at Da Nang in case things get too serious for the Spads to handle. And, finally, the Sky Hook Herkys will be airborne right on our side of the fence, and they promise to make the pickup within twenty minutes."

"That sounds all well and good," Reese replied. "But what about the extract? We may have to haul ass out of there at a moment's notice."

"They will use the Jolly Green for an emergency extract on your call, and the Spads will fly cover for you on that, too."

Reese studied the map and photos for another long moment. "I'd like to bring my people in now and go over this with them," he said.

The team listened carefully as Reese went over the details of the plan. He handed them the photos so they could acquaint themselves with what the area really looked like. Briefing with maps had drawbacks in that maps didn't always accurately show the vegetation and minor ground features of the target area. After giving out the radio call signs and frequencies, Reese asked if there were any questions, but there were none. Even though they were going into Laos, the mission was very straightforward.

"If this thing goes the way we've planned," Reese concluded, "it'll be a piece of cake, as our Brit SAS friends say. But if there's a fuck-up, all bets are off. Everyone's going to have to stay on their toes until we hit the extract bird."

Kowalski grinned. "We'd better stay on our toes, *Dai Uy,* until we get back to Dak Sang and a cold beer."

"You pull this one off, Sergeant," Snow said, "and the beer will be on me."

"You got a deal, sir. Just as long as it ain't Miller."

A few minutes later one of CCC's operation sergeants stuck his head in the doorway of the briefing room. "The bird's waiting on the pad," he announced.

"Saddle up!" Reese said, reaching for his loaded rucksack and CAR-15.

Snow helped him into his ruck. "I'll walk out with you."

The chopper sitting on the helipad, its main rotor spinning, wasn't one of the mat-black sterile Huey Slicks CCC normally used for clandestine cross-border missions. This was a hulking machine almost three times the size of the Bell Huey, painted in two shades of mat-green-and-tan camouflage with a gray belly.

Carried on the government inventory sheets as a Sikorsky HH-53 Sea Stallion, this massive machine with its six-bladed rotor was known as the Jolly Green Giant. Normally used for Air Force Search and Rescue (SAR) missions deep over enemy territory, the Sikorsky ship had been chosen to carry Reese's team into action instead of a Huey because of its high speed, longer range and greater carrying capability. It would have taken two Hueys to carry Reese's men and their equipment.

Reese hung back while his team clambered on board the chopper. "I've got a real antsy feeling about this, sir," he said. "So make sure you pass on anything you hear from MACV or the blue suiters."

"You can count on that," Snow said, clapping Reese on the back. "Good luck."

Reese shot him a thumbs-up and, bending over to shield his face from the red dirt thrown up by the rotor blast, scrambled aboard the Jolly Green Giant. Inside the rear fuselage the team quickly buckled themselves into the canvas troop seats while the aircrew quickly stowed the Sky Hook equipment and tied it down.

One of the Air Force crewmen handed Reese a spare flight helmet. The SF captain plugged the intercom cord into the jack behind his seat and put it on. After checking that everyone was strapped in, he keyed the mike. "We're go back here," he called up to the pilot.

"Roger," the pilot answered, twisting his throttle up against the stop. "We're lifting off now."

With the twin 3,080-horsepower turbines screaming the pilot pulled pitch to the six-bladed main rotor, and the Jolly Green Giant rose from the pad and turned northwest. As the chopper climbed, Reese settled back against the webbing of the seat for the long ride to the Laotian landing zone.

Most of the others leaned back and tried to nap, but Reese's mind was racing. Even though the mission had been put together quickly, he knew everything possible to ensure its success had been done. But he still had a nagging feeling that this wasn't going to be as easy as it appeared. There were too many things about the loss of the Spectre that didn't make sense.

First and foremost was the fact that the MiG had strayed so far from North Vietnam to shoot down this particular aircraft. Why hadn't it shot down any other

American aircraft while it was in Laos? Why had it gone all that way for a single kill? From the transcript he had read of the Spectre pilot's panicked radio transmissions, that was exactly what it had been—a kill, a surgical assassination of the prototype gunship one engine at a time.

If the NVA had wanted to ensure that the plane was taken out, why shoot it down that way? Why not simply take it out with an air-to-air missile and scatter the pieces all over southern Laos? That was the one question no one had been able to answer to his satisfaction. He had a bad feeling he'd find the answer as soon as they reached the crash site.

Then there was the report from the attempted Sandy Flight rescue that three of the crewmen had survived, but hadn't been rescued. Sandy Lead had reported that radio contact had been lost and that no one had been seen at the crash site. What had happened to those three men?

Reese figured they had been policed up by the enemy. If that was so, there would likely be a reception committee waiting for his team, too.

6

Steel Tiger, Laos

The insertion went like a well-practiced training exercise back at the JFK Special Warfare Center. While Reese's team waited inside the open rear ramp door, the Jolly Green Giant dropped to a low hover a few meters over the LZ. Seven rappelling ropes hung from the chopper's ramp, and the team members were already hooked up to the ropes. The instant the pilot flared out to kill the chopper's forward momentum, they dropped out of the door. Under the watchful eyes of the Jolly Green's door gunners they were on the ground safely in seconds and fanning out in the bush.

Unclipping his rappelling rope, Reese gave the door gunner a high sign as he raced for cover. The Jolly Green immediately accelerated into the sky. In seconds the big chopper was out of sight, keeping low to the ground until it was well clear of the area. For the first few minutes the men remained motionless in their hiding places, looking and listening for any sign of the enemy.

When he was satisfied that the area was clear, Reese stood up and, using hand and arm signals, sent the seven men into patrol formation. Reese took up the point position himself, with Santelli on slack behind him. Kowalski went back to the drag position, with Hotchkiss backing him up. Wilson, Torres and Whiskey, the Nung interpreter, stayed in the middle of the formation as Reese moved out on a compass heading of 027 degrees.

Although the insertion had gone like clockwork, it didn't ease Reese's mind. If anything, it put him even more on edge. The terrain in this part of Steel Tiger was flat and covered with light scrub. The team should have been able to move fairly quickly, but Reese was taking no chances and moved cautiously from one clump of scrub to the next. One reason for the caution was that their jungle camouflage tiger suits and face paint made them stand out against the lighter greens of the plain's vegetation. Another reason was that he had an itchy feeling that they weren't alone.

This part of Laos was supposed to be crawling with NVA, and the recon photos clearly indicated that they had been at the crash site. But so far none of the aircraft had reported seeing any signs of the enemy on the way in to the target area, and that bothered him. He liked his NVA out in the open where he could see them.

While Reese was apprehensive about the situation, Santelli was in his element. As the slack man on the patrol, Santelli's main job was to be Reese's second pair of eyes, constantly watching for anything the point man might have missed. If they did make contact, Santelli would rush to Reese's aid and, if Reese was hit, would take over and lead the fight. Walking either the point or slack position was nerve-racking, but this was what the wiry young officer lived for—the pulse-pounding, adrenaline high of stalking danger with the chance of the orgasmic release of a firefight at the end.

Jack Santelli hadn't always been a combat junkie. As a teenager growing up in a predominantly Italian-American neighborhood in the Bronx, he had shown no particular signs of bloodthirstiness. His family ran a prosperous fruit and vegetable business and had expected him to join them in it when he graduated from high school. He had other ideas, however. To the complete dismay of his family, Santelli enlisted in the Army immediately upon graduation.

While still in basic training, he was selected for Officer Candidate School. Upon being commissioned, he volunteered for Airborne, Ranger and Special Forces training in turn. When he arrived in-country for his first tour, he was just one more young officer with no combat experience. But that changed with his first firefight, and the past four months had addicted him to the thrill of combat.

There were no reluctant warriors in the U.S. Army Special Forces. Men who had lingering doubts about themselves or the risks of combat never made it through the rigorous training to be awarded the coveted Green Beret. The Special Forces men in Vietnam proved their courage time and again, almost on a daily basis, but not all of them were afflicted with Santelli's fierce hunger for danger.

While Reese and his veteran sergeants hoped for a quick, successful conclusion to this mission, Santelli almost hoped that something would go wrong. Not anything serious enough to endanger the lives of the team, of course, but something that would give him a chance to experience the indescribable highs of combat once more.

After half an hour on the move, Reese called a halt on a slight rise. As the others fanned out in the bush, Reese took out his field glasses and studied the wreck in the distance. The crashed Spectre lay at the southern edge of the plain a mile or so from a small hill. The nose of the plane was crushed, and the left wing had been twisted and bent back against the fuselage by the impact. The rear ramp door was down, but he couldn't see inside the darkened fuselage. There was no movement, no sign of life around the wreck. Nor, for that matter, was there any movement anywhere within his field of vision.

"How does it look?" Santelli asked.

"Quiet as a tomb."

Reese motioned for Torres to bring the radio up. Taking the handset, he called Hillsboro, the C-130 airborne command post that was coordinating the operation. "Hillsboro, this is Gray Ghost One One, over."

"Ghost One One, Hillsboro. I read you loud and clear. Send your traffic."

"This is One One, I have the wreckage in sight, but there is negative sign of your survivors. Over."

"Hillsboro, roger."

"We'll be at the site in two zero. Alert Sky Hook, over."

"Hillsboro, wilco, out."

Handing the radio handset back to Torres, Reese signaled for the team to move out again. When they were still a hundred meters out, Reese halted and scanned the area around the wreck with his field glasses once more. He spotted a patch of what looked like olive-drab cloth in the grass a few meters to one side of the plane. Focusing his glasses, he saw that a figure in an olive-drab flight suit lay crumpled stiffly on the ground. The figure didn't move, and Reese decided it was the body of one of the dead crewmen he had seen on the recon photos.

"See anything?" Santelli asked.

"Just one of the bodies."

"How are we going to get them out?"

"We're not," Reese answered. "The Air Force is going to take care of that after we get that fire control gear out of there."

"Poor bastards."

Reese handed his glasses to Santelli. "I'm taking Ski and going in for a closer look. Don't forget that there's supposed to be three of our guys somewhere around here, so make sure of what you shoot at."

"Be careful, Captain."

"You got that shit right," Reese said as he flicked the selector switch of his CAR-15 off safety. "It's a little too quiet out there."

Signaling for Kowalski to follow him, Reese left Santelli and the rest of the team in a fire support position to cover them. Reese and Kowalski slowly approached the wreck. One of them would move ahead a few meters while the other covered him. It was a slow way to approach the wreck, but Reese was willing to take his time.

The first indication that someone had been there before them was that the bloated body of the first crewman they reached had been stripped of his boots, socks and survival vest. When Reese looked closer, he saw the gaping hole in the man's chest where one of the MiG's 23 mm armor-piercing rounds had smashed through him.

With Kowalski covering him Reese crept the last twenty meters to the smashed cockpit. The door just aft of the cockpit was half-open, but he couldn't see much inside the darkened fuselage. He was heading for the rear of the plane and the open ramp door when he spotted a flash of movement in the bush a hundred meters away.

Signaling Kowalski to take cover, Reese fell flat on his face in the grass, bringing his CAR-15 into firing position. He was crawling for cover against the side of the plane when a burst of AK fire cut through the grass to his right front. Instinctively he triggered off a long burst of 5.56 mm where he had seen movement moments before. Answering AK fire snapped over his head.

From his fire support position Santelli sprang into action with the first burst of AK fire. As the rest of the team opened up to lay down a base of fire to try to protect Reese and Kowalski, Santelli snatched up the radio handset. "Give me the FAC push!" he yelled to Torres.

The RTO quickly switched the PRC-77 over to the FM frequency for the airborne forward air controller orbiting out of sight in his small Cessna O-2A Skymaster spotter plane. The twin-boom O-2 was fondly nicknamed the Push Pull because it had one engine in front and another at the rear. For the same reason it was also sometimes derisively called the Suck and Blow.

Whatever its nickname, the O-2 was the perfect plane for the dangerous job of Forward Air Control. It was fairly fast, extremely maneuverable and could be armed, which meant it could protect itself. The pilots who flew it loved it as much as the men on the ground did who depended on it to call the Tac Air in to save their ass.

"His call sign's Billboard," Torres reminded the lieutenant.

"Billboard, Billboard, this is Gray Ghost One Two. We're being hit! Get those Spads down here fast!"

"This is Billboard Four Five," the FAC calmly answered. "Roger your contact. Give me a target and pop smoke."

Snatching a smoke grenade from the side of his ammo pouch, Santelli pulled the pin and tossed it out behind him. The fuse ignited the grenade with a pop, and thick red smoke billowed into the air.

"I have red smoke," the FAC radioed.

"Roger cherry," Santelli called back. "The target is that line of bush nine hundred meters north of the smoke."

"Billboard, roger. Let me call the Spads."

The FAC switched his radio over to the UHF channel and keyed the mike to call the flight of A-1 Spads he had on-station. "Gypsy Lead, this is Billboard Four Five. I have business for you. Gray Ghost is taking fire and needs you to take care of it for him."

"Gypsy Lead, roger," the Spad pilot called back. "We'll be there in zero two. Give me some smoke."

"Roger, I'm rolling in now."

The Push Pull pilot advanced his throttle and winged over into a dive. This was where the FACs earned their combat pay. While the Spads could drop their bombs on Santelli's radioed description of the enemy's location, their runs would be much more accurate if the FAC could drop a Willie Peter marking rocket for the pilots to use as an aiming point.

Alerted by the sound of the diving plane, the NVA directed some of their fire at the FAC. Glowing green AK tracers raced up at the small plane as it bore down on them. When the FAC saw the winking of muzzle-flashes aimed at him, he triggered his own armament. For this mission the plane had been fitted with two 7.62 mm minigun pods under the wing, and they returned fire at three thousand rounds a minute, spraying the bush with hot lead and keeping the enemy heads down.

From fifteen hundred meters out the FAC triggered his marking rocket pod under the plane's wing. The 2.75-inch folding-fin rocket left the pod with a whoosh and sped for the ground, trailing dirty white smoke. When it hit the ground, it exploded in a ball of white smoke directly in the middle of the line of bush.

Racking his plane around to clear the area, the FAC keyed his mike. "Gypsy Lead, smoke out."

"Four Five, this is Lead. FAC in sight and I have your smoke."

"Roger, you're cleared in hot. Make your attack from east to west along that line of bush. The friendlies are by the wreck and nine hundred meters to the south."

"Lead, roger. Rolling in now. Snake and nape on the way."

On the ground Reese heard the rising howl of the powerful piston engines as two of the Spads dived on the FAC's smoke marker, and he flattened himself. The howl rose to a scream as attack planes bore down on the target, the 20 mm cannons in their wings blazing to suppress enemy ground fire. Reese pressed himself even tighter against the ground and brought his hands up over his ears.

As the lead plane pulled out of its dive, two olive-drab 750-pound Snake Eye-retarded bombs dropped off the underwing pylons. Fins at the tail of the bombs immediately snapped open, acting as parachutes to slow the bomb and allow the Spad to get away before the ordnance hit the ground and detonated.

Seconds later the bombs hit within ten feet of the smoke marker. The concussion lifted Reese and Kowalski off the ground and slammed them back down again. Dirt and bits of scrub showered down on them.

The smoke hadn't cleared before the second Spad delivered two 125-gallon tanks of napalm right on top of the bomb craters. The jellied gasoline ignited with a whoosh, filling the air with the stench of burning fuel as a boiling fireball thirty feet wide and a hundred feet long devoured both the stunned NVA and the bomb-blasted bush around them.

Reese felt the searing blast of superheated air wash over him, instantly drying the sweat from his soaked tiger suit. He held his breath until he felt the normal heat of the sun on his skin again. After the napalm-heated air, it felt almost cool. This was the closest he had ever been to the receiving end of a napalm attack, and he never wanted to get closer.

The fireball died down, but the bush still blazed as the O-2 dropped low over the target again. The FAC drew no ground fire and wasn't able to see anyone moving in the burning bush. He pulled up and circled over the smoke plume. "Ghost One Two," he radioed. "This is Billboard. I don't see any movement. I think we got 'em all."

"Roger, Billboard," Santelli answered. "Thanks."

"No sweat," the FAC answered. "If you need any more, just give me a call. Billboard clear."

Reese and Kowalski were scouting the blasted enemy position, looking for NVA survivors, when Santelli and the rest of the team joined up with them. The bushfire was still sending a thick column of smoke into the sky and raining fine ash down on them.

"Thanks for the assist," Reese told Santelli. "If they'd held their fire for just a few more minutes, they'd have gotten both of us."

Santelli brushed ash from his face. "It was nice to have the fly-boys show up on time for a change. The next time I get to Da Nang, I'll have to buy that FAC a beer.''

"When you do," Reese said, "I'll pay."

"What's the body count in there?"

Reese shrugged. "Hard to tell. I've found a couple, but you'd better sweep that whole area. We don't need any more interruptions."

While the team quickly searched the NVA bodies that hadn't been incinerated and collected their weapons, Reese ducked inside the Spectre to take a look at the gear they had come to secure. He came back out quickly, a grim look on his face.

"What's wrong, *Dai Uy?*" Torres asked when he saw his expression.

Reese ignored the RTO as he took the radio handset from where it was clipped to his assault harness. "Hillsboro, Gray Ghost One One, over," Reese radioed.

"Hillsboro, go ahead."

"This is One One. We've got a slight problem down here. Someone grabbed the package before we could get here. The wreck's been stripped clean. Over."

There was a long pause before Hillsboro answered, "Roger, One One. Understand the package is gone. Stand by, please."

7

Steel Tiger, Laos

"Now what do we do, Captain?" Santelli asked, taking his boonie hat off and running his fingers through his short-cropped hair.

Reese's green eyes quickly scanned their surroundings. "We wait here till we hear what SOG wants us to do next."

"That may not be too fucking healthy," Santelli said. He was ready for another fight, but only one that he could fight on his own terms. "With that air strike every Dink within a ten-mile radius of this place has got to know we're here, and this isn't the easiest place in the world to defend. Let's pull back and find a place where we can dig in if we need to."

"I can't do that," Reese explained. "We've got to stay with the plane until they release us, so you'd better put some security out. And keep that FAC on the horn. We may need that guy again real quick."

"Roger that."

While Santelli went to organize their security, Reese had Silk Wilson, the medic, Torres, and Whiskey, the Nung, start collecting the American dead and preparing them for later evacuation. One of the first bodies they came to was the one that had lost its boots and socks.

"Why would a Commie want to take this guy's boots?" Wilson asked as he took one of the man's dog tags from the chain around his neck. "No NVA I ever saw would be able to wear them. This guy's much too big."

"Maybe they had a Red Chinese adviser with them," Torres said. "I've heard that some of those guys are almost as tall as we are."

"No, *Trung Si.*" The Nung interpreter shook his head. "They too big for Chinese man, too." The Nung, who was five foot ten, placed his boot next to the dead man's foot. The tip of his boot didn't even come to the base of the airman's bare toes.

"Maybe they took them for some sort of trophy," Torres mused.

"Beats the shit outta me," Wilson replied. "But let's get these guys policed up before they start to stink."

All the bodies bore severe wounds. The MiG's AP cannon shells, designed to punch through steel armor plate, had done frightening damage to human flesh. One of the bodies had to be collected in pieces, and all of them had started to bloat in the sun.

KOWALSKI, in the bush behind the wreck, had a good view of the surrounding territory. With so few of them to secure the area, he was alone at his post.

"Hey!" a voice sounded from the clump of bush to his left.

Kowalski spun around, his CAR-15 leveled and his finger on the trigger.

"Don't shoot!" the voice said. "I'm an American!"

"Come out with your hands up over your head."

Slowly a man stood up, his hands held high. Kowalski saw that the man was an American, but he held his CAR on him as he motioned him closer in case there was an enemy behind him. "Are you from that plane?"

The man nodded. "Damn, am I glad to see you."

Kowalski lowered his submachine gun when he saw that the man was alone. "Come on. I'll take you to my captain."

Kowalski found Reese at the back of the wreck where he and Torres had set up the radio and established their temporary CP on the plane's open ramp door. "Got a visitor for you, sir," he said.

Reese turned and saw a stocky blond man in a rumpled, dirty Air Force flight suit with the gold oak leaves of a major sewn on the shoulders.

"Hammer," the Air Force major said, extending his hand. "Nails Hammer. I was the fire control officer on that bird." He turned his head slightly toward the wreck.

Reese shook Hammer's hand. "Captain Mike Reese, Special Forces Team A-410."

The major quickly looked around. "You didn't find a couple more of my crewmen, did you?"

"I've got some bodies, but you're the only survivor we've found so far."

"Let me see the bodies," Hammer said through clenched teeth.

Reese led him to where Wilson had laid the casualties out. Hammer quickly scanned the bloated faces. "Nope, they're not here."

"Who are you talking about?"

"Sergeant Kegan, the crew chief," Hammer said. "And Airman Jones, one of the gunners. They were here when I went to radio for help. The gunner was hurt, and Kegan stayed behind to help him."

Reese shook his head. "The Dinks must have found them."

A look of anguish passed over Hammer's face. "Fuckin' bastards."

"Are you hurt?" Reese asked. "I've got a medic here if you need him."

"No." Hammer shook his head. "I'm okay. I just bumped my head when we landed."

Reese motioned for Wilson to bring his aid bag, and he hurried over. "Let's have a look at your head, Major."

When Wilson saw Hammer eyeing his M-16 and the grenades on his ammo pouches, he explained, "I'm the team medic, but everyone on an A-team is a combat soldier first."

"Shoot the bastards first, then patch 'em up. Right?"

Wilson grinned. "That's about it, sir. Now let's take a look at your head."

The medic took the flyer's pulse, checked the swelling on the back of his head and shone a light in his eyes to check his reflexes. "That's a nasty bump, sir," he said. "But as far as I can tell, it doesn't look like you have a concussion. If you start having trouble with blurred vision, though, let me know immediately." He rummaged around in his aid bag and came out with two pills. "Here, take these. They'll help the pain and take the swelling down."

"What are they?"

"Aspirin."

Hammer almost smiled. "Take two and call me in the morning, right?"

"I don't want to give you codeine, Major. It'll make you drowsy."

Hammer took the pills and washed them down with water from the canteen Wilson offered.

Reese returned and said, "Look, Major, we've got a Sky Hook bird on-station and we can get you out of here in less than half an hour."

"No!" Hammer shook his head violently. "I've got to try to find my people."

"That may be a little difficult, sir," Reese said carefully. "We don't have any hard information about who has captured them or where they are being taken."

"You can try to track them down, can't you?" Hammer asked. "You Green Berets do that sort of thing all the time, don't you?"

"Yes, sir. We may be able to do that. But I have to wait and see what my headquarters wants us to do next."

Reese could see Hammer's jaw clench even tighter and the pulse pound in his neck, but the flyer wisely kept from pressuring Reese to go after his missing crewmen.

"I'm sorry, sir," Reese said. "I understand how you feel, but we're under direct orders from MACV on this mission. I can't undertake anything on my own without clearing it through them first. But I promise I'll talk to them about your men."

"Thanks," Hammer replied.

"It's the best I can do," Reese said.

A FEW MILES NORTH of the crash site Major Yermolav had seen the American ground-attack aircraft swarm over the downed Spectre and saw the smoke rising from the air strike. He was certain the Yankees had sent a team in to examine the wreck and they had come under fire from the North Vietnamese ground troops Vinh had left behind. There was no way he could determine the outcome of the battle from where he was, but he knew the handful of men the NVA officer had there wouldn't have fared well under the kind of concentrated air attack the American Air Force was famous for.

Yermolav really didn't care if the North Vietnamese had survived, but he hoped they had inflicted some damage on the Americans or at least had held them up long enough that they couldn't pursue him until he could get away.

Now that Yermolav had a decent pair of boots to wear, his feet didn't hurt, and he was setting a blistering pace northward. Burdened with the fire control equipment and the wounded Yankee, the short-legged North Vietnamese were almost forced to run to keep up with him. But that didn't bother the Russian at all. As far as he was concerned, it served the little bastards right.

When they had been on the way for more than half an hour, Vinh asked if he could dispose of the wounded Yankee so that his men wouldn't have to carry him as well as the captured equipment. Yermolav refused. The Russian wasn't at all concerned about the American's life. But he thought the crewman might provide valuable information about the weapons systems on the Spectre. The Soviet air force had sent him to this godforsaken place with orders to get every scrap of information about the new gunship he possibly could. That included any surviving aircrew, so Vinh's men would just have to sacrifice a little more sweat for their cause and carry the wounded American as long as he could be kept alive.

Vinh's unit didn't have a medic with them, but the other captured Yankee flyer was tending to his comrade and did have the medical bag he had taken from the crash.

"Get them moving again, Vinh," Yermolav growled.

Keeping his thin face completely expressionless, the North Vietnamese officer ordered his men to continue the march.

BACK IN KONTOUM Major Snow had been informed about the situation at the Spectre crash site and was in communication with the folks at MACV-SOG Headquarters at the Tan Son Nhut Air Force Base outside Saigon while they decided what to do. Once more the Hungarian officer had been reminded of the greatest of all military truisms: no plan ever survives the initial contact with the enemy.

Despite the great speed with which it had been put together, this had been a simple but good plan. Drop in, grab the gear, get the hell out. No one, however, had considered that the enemy might get to the wreck first and salvage the classified equipment themselves. Now MACV was back to square one.

This new information proved that the downing of the high-tech gunship, systematically shot down one engine at a time, had been done for a specific purpose. Now they knew what that purpose was. The only question was how to recover the plane's missing black boxes.

While he waited for MACV to decide what Reese should do next, Snow stared out the window, his mind methodically reviewing the information he had, trying to formulate another plan.

"What do you think, Iceman?" Lieutenant Colonel Newman asked. "Is there anything we can do to salvage this mess? Can you pull another one of your famous rabbits out of the hat?"

Snow walked to the big map of Laos pinned on the wall. The operations officer was skeptical about recovering the equipment, but he wasn't about to give up. He hadn't gained his widely known reputation as the master of SOG's clandestine operations by backing down from what seemed to be an impossible situation.

Snow's first fight against communism had been in Budapest during the Hungarian Revolution of 1956. That valiant but vain struggle had been against impossible odds. Hungarian freedom fighters armed with a few captured weapons and gasoline-filled bottles had faced down Russian JS III heavy tanks and, for a while, had been able to hold them off. Faced with repeated assaults by Soviet armored units, Snow and his handful of followers, most of them college students and Hungarian army deserters, had fought until their captured ammunition was gone. Then they had fought with paving stones until they could fight no more.

Like that fight in the streets of Budapest, everything was going against him again this time. But now he wasn't alone. The vast military power of the United States Army and Air Force was backing him up. And the North Vietnamese army wasn't half the opponent the Russians had been.

"The main thing we have going for us," Snow said quietly in his precise English, "is that Reese's men are already in place on the ground. If we can get some idea where the enemy is taking that stuff, we can send our men after it."

"Isn't that a real long shot? Laos is a big country, and there are a lot of places to hide."

"It is big," Snow agreed, "and it is crawling with NVA. But if we can get a little cooperation from the

Air Force, maybe we can still pull this off, or at least ensure that the equipment is destroyed.''

"I've got a feeling the blue suiters will give us damn near anything we ask for. What do you want?''

Snow stared at the map. "First off, we need another Blackbird run over Steel Tiger between the crash site and the North Vietnamese border. Next, I need a constant radar watch over the same area with air cover on ramp alert. If the NVA puts another chopper in the air anywhere around there, I need someone to splash it instantly.''

He turned back to the colonel. "Finally, and most important, I need to keep whoever has that stuff on foot so we have a chance to catch up with them. To do that the Air Force will have to go all-out for us.''

"Like I said, I think we can count on that. What exactly do you have in mind?''

Snow's finger traced a circle around a section of the map. "I need this area to be completely interdicted. I need them to blast anything on wheels going in or out of this area. Boats, too.'' He tapped the thin blue line that marked the trace of the Xe Ban Foi River running north to south in eastern Laos. "That will insure that the NVA stay on foot while we send the hounds after them.''

"What do you mean?''

"Reese's men aren't the only assets we have in that part of Laos,'' Snow said. "It may be time to contact the Laos Section in SOG and see about freeing up some other forces to help.''

"You think they'll buy it?''

Snow shrugged. "That depends on how badly the Air Force wants that stuff back."

Newman laughed. "They want it all right. You can count on that."

"Then we might be able to pull this one off."

8

Steel Tiger, Laos

It was over an hour before CCC got back to Reese with MACV's decision. The radio message was sent in three-letter code groups, and it took Reese á long time to decode them with his SOI. After reading the lengthy message, he called his team together for a briefing.

"Okay," he said, spreading his map out on the open ramp door. "Here's the drill. We're going after the equipment." He glanced over at Major Hammer. "And the missing aircrew. MACV wants all of them back ASAP."

The Air Force officer looked grim, but he was ready to go after his captured crewmen. He had armed himself with an AK-47 assault rifle from one of the enemy dead and was wearing the NVA's chest pack magazine carrier hanging from a field belt. He had also gathered two canteens from the wreckage and had tied a triangular olive-drab cloth bandage from the plane's first-aid kit around his head as a sweat rag.

"This is going to be a fucking wild-goose chase," Reese said. "All we know is that they've taken that gear and they need to get it to North Vietnam fast. But when Sandy splashed their chopper, that put them on foot. The Iceman thinks they'll try to carry the equipment up to here—'' his finger stabbed the map ''—one of the main roads of the Ho Chi Minh Trail, then try to put it on a truck heading north.

"To keep them from doing that the Air Force is going to swarm all over the Trail in this area like flies on shit and blast everything they see on wheels. But it's still going to be a crap shoot. If they can keep these guys on foot, we'll have a chance to catch up with them. If they can get to a truck and drive past the planes, we're screwed.

"To give us a hand they're going to run another Blackbird recon to search for the guys we're after. Until then, we're going to start after them and see if we can follow their trail. While they're loaded down with the gear and the prisoners, we're traveling light, and we should be able to catch up with them before too long.

"The tracks Kowalski found indicate they're heading northeast, and the map says there's a little village about eight klicks in that direction, so we're going to go check it out. Beyond that, I don't know what we'll do. For now we're just going to have to cover ground as fast as we can until we can develop more hard intelligence about where they've gone." Reese looked at each member of his team. "Any questions?"

"When are we going?" Hammer growled.

Reese looked up. "One thing first, Major. I know you're real gung ho to join us, but I've got to warn you that this isn't going to be a walk in the sun. This is going to be a real hump, and you're going to have to keep up with us. We can't afford to hang back because you can't hack it when the going gets rough. And once we're under way, I can't stop and call for Sky Hook to extract you.''

Hammer's jaw clenched even tighter. "Don't worry about me, Captain. This is one fucking blue suiter who can keep up with you super soldier guys."

Reese studied his face. "I sure as hell hope so, Major. And another thing, sir," Reese said, eyeing Hammer's AK. "Do you know how to use that thing?"

Hammer's right thumb reached out to the selector switch on the side of the assault rifle right above the pistol grip. "Thirty-round magazine. Up for safe, middle position for single shot and all the way down for full-auto. It climbs like a motherfucker on full-auto, though, so you have to fire three-round bursts to keep it on target."

"Where'd you learn that?"

"I've always been kind of a gun nut, and we have several of these back at Udorn that we use for target practice."

"That's good, Major," Reese said. "But remember that the rule of engagement is that you don't shoot unless we shoot first."

"Call me Nails, damn it," Hammer snapped. "Until this thing's over we can drop the military protocol bullshit."

Reese grinned. "That's fine with me. And you can call me Reese."

Hammer relaxed a little. "Okay, Reese. When are we leaving?"

"Right now."

Hammer smiled. "Good. Then how about a little lunch? I haven't had anything to eat since yesterday afternoon."

Reese pulled his ruck over to him. "What's your pleasure? H and MFs or Lurps?"

Hammer frowned. "What are you talking about?"

Reese grinned. "Canned ham and limas, or freeze-dried rice and monkey meat."

"Jesus!" Hammer shuddered theatrically. "No fucking wonder you guys are crazy enough to run all over Laos. Look at what you eat!"

"How about some beanie wienies, Major?" Santelli said, holding out an opened can and a white plastic spoon. "They're not too bad with a little Tabasco."

"Thanks," he said, taking the can. "That sounds a little more appetizing."

Santelli handed the flyer another opened can to go with the first. "Here's the cheese and crackers that go along with that, Major."

Hammer, stuffing his mouth full of beans and franks, accepted the can from Santelli. He swallowed, then said, "Thanks, and don't call me major. My name's Nails."

"Roger that, Major."

When everyone had eaten, they tossed the empty cans inside the wreck and got back into their rucks. Backing the team a safe distance away from the wreck, Santelli ran inside the open fuselage and tossed a thermite grenade into a pool of JP-4 jet fuel. The fuel ignited with a whoosh, and Santelli ran back out. In seconds the wreck was ablaze from end to end and the ammunition for the guns started cooking off.

"Okay," Reese said, "let's get it."

The team moved out with Kowalski on point and Whiskey on slack, backing him up. Hotchkiss watched their backtrail, while Reese stayed with Torres so he could be close to the radio. The sun would be down in an hour and a half, but according to his map, they should be able to reach the village before dark.

As they moved from the foothills onto the Laotian plain, the broken scrub changed to cleared fields and rice paddies. The fields weren't in cultivation, and from the look of them hadn't been for quite some time. The presence of so many North Vietnamese troops in the area around the Ho Chi Minh Trail had severely affected the lives of the Laotian peasants. From the intelligence reports Reese had read, large areas of southern Laos had been completely depopulated over the past three years. Many Laotians had been killed, but most had been displaced or pressed into the North Vietnamese labor gangs that tried to keep the Ho Chi Minh Trail repaired in the face of repeated American bombings.

Whatever the reason the natives had left, their desertion gave the once-fertile land an eerie feel and put Reese even more on edge. The Iceman's briefing had indicated that the village he was approaching was still populated, but it wasn't known if it was in enemy hands or not. They would have to find that out for themselves once they got there.

Now that they had broken out into clear terrain and had good fields of observation all around them, Reese shifted his formation into a column and moved up on the point with Kowalski to set as fast a pace as he could. As they hurried along, Hammer walked in the center of the column with Torres and Wilson.

The black medic studied the Air Force officer as they marched along. For a man who wasn't infantry-trained and who had just survived a plane crash, Hammer wasn't doing too badly on his first patrol. "How're you feeling, Major?" Wilson asked.

Hammer grinned and wiped the sweat from the back of his neck. "I'm doing just fine for a fly-boy, Doc. Don't worry. I'll be able to keep up with you guys."

Wilson noticed the rime of dried sweat under the arms and down the back of the major's uniform. Swinging his aid bag around so that he could dig into it, he found a plastic bottle of pink pills and held them out. "Here, I want you to take two of these at least three times a day with water."

"What are they?"

"Salt tabs," Wilson explained. "As much as you're sweating, you need to replace the salt or you're going to have a heat stroke."

Hammer took the pills. "Right, I remember that from survival training, but I thought that only applied to the desert."

Wilson smiled and offered his canteen. "You can have a heat stroke here just as fast as you can in the desert. Faster, in fact, because with the high humidity, you don't feel the water loss as much.''

"You're the doc.'' Hammer shook out two of the pills and washed them down with water from Wilson's canteen. "Thanks.''

"I also have more aspirin if your head's hurting you,'' Wilson offered.

"I'm okay now, but I'll let you know if I need anything.''

IN THE MIDDLE of the NVA formation Master Sergeant Kegan walked alongside the litter carrying the wounded Airman Jones as they hurried through the empty fields. The NVA hadn't tied Kegan's hands, but the noose around his neck limited his movements and effectively prevented him from running away.

Not that he would have tried to run, however. As long as Jones was alive, he would stay with him and do what he could to help him. But there was little he could do for the gunner. His leg wound had been bandaged, and Kegan had given him a couple of shots of morphine, but that wasn't going to keep him from losing the leg. Kegan was an old Asia hand, and he knew that unless Jones got to a hospital within the next day or so, he'd lose the leg to one of the tropical infections that always followed a serious wound.

Kegan didn't have the slightest idea where they were going. From the moment they had been surprised and captured, the NVA had said little to them. Even the Russian air force officer had said nothing. Kegan had been surprised to see a round eye with the enemy, but he recognized the Russian uniform and insignia from the know-your-enemy classes at his duty stations in Germany.

At first he hadn't been able to figure out what the hell a Russian was doing in Laos. It was well-known that there were Russian air force advisers in North Vietnam, but this guy was a long way from Hanoi. When he saw the Russian supervising the removal of the fire control and sensor gear from the wreck, Kegan realized the guy was some kind of technical expert and was stealing the guts of the high-tech gunship so that the Soviets could build one of their own.

This pissed off the Spectre's crew chief more than their shooting him down. The risk of getting shot down was what war in the air was all about. The enemy stealing bits and pieces from the wreckage, however, offended his sense of fair play. If the Russians wanted to have a gunship, let them design one on their own. Maybe they could convert one of their Antonov An-12 assault transports, which were more or less a rip-off of the Herky Bird, anyway. Kegan had to focus on survival and helping Jones, but if he got half a chance to destroy the captured equipment, he'd go for it.

After two hours on the march, Yermolav was a little footsore, even with his new American boots, and was glad to reach the small Laotian village. A security squad of North Vietnamese troops ran on ahead. By the time the Russian reached the first of the cluster of small bamboo huts, the villagers had all been rounded up and were waiting.

The village headman spoke some Vietnamese, and Vinh's sergeant made it clear to him that the Laotians were to feed the North Vietnamese. He also made it clear, by placing the children under armed guard, that the villagers had better not try anything foolish. While Yermolav and Vinh rested under the awning of the headman's house, the villagers hurried to provide food for their visitors.

The headman sent two of his young women to the officers to offer them hot tea or anything else they wanted. The headman had been through this routine with the North Vietnamese many times, and knew that anything he could do to put them at ease would benefit the village in the long run. They no longer had any young men for the NVA to press into their work gangs, but the village would survive by being friendly. The two women who brought the tea had lost their husbands to the war and were willing to make the sacrifice for the good of their village. To the women's relief, however, neither Vinh nor Yermolav was interested in that kind of hospitality, though they did drink the tea.

The food was readied quickly and, while it was meager fare, mostly steamed greens and shreds of chicken meat, there was plenty of rice. Yermolav could eat rice without aggravating his stomach condition any further, so he ate several bowls.

The Russian was just finishing when Vinh approached him. "Comrade Major," the Vietnamese lieutenant said, "it will be dark soon and we need to get moving."

"No." The Russian shook his head. "We're going to stay here tonight. I need to sleep."

Vinh stood tall and unconsciously puffed his chest out. Placed in charge of the ground element of this operation, he'd had about all he could take from this fat, foul-smelling Russian long nose. Vinh had gone to a Soviet university and was no stranger to the ways of these hairy barbarian comrades. Even though he had lived with them for two years, he had never become used to their overwhelming arrogance and their complete lack of respect for anyone who wasn't Russian, particularly for anyone whose skin wasn't white.

"Sorry, Comrade Major," Vinh said firmly. "I am responsible for the security of this equipment, and for your own safety, as well. While this area is under the control of the People's Army, there are still gangs of roaming bandits in the pay of the Yankees. Since our radios were in the helicopter, and there is no way to call for assistance, I insist that we keep on the move until we can reach a larger unit of my army or some transportation we can use."

Maybe Vinh had a point, Yermolav thought. The Americans obviously knew he had salvaged their classified equipment from the Spectre. The action back at the crash site proved that. Not only was there the danger of running into local guerrilla forces allied with the Americans—the "bandits," as Vinh called them—there was always the possibility that the American troops were searching for him, as well. He knew about the exploits of their Special Forces long-range patrol units, some of which had ventured far into North Vietnam. Maybe he had better keep on the move just to be safe.

"All right," he said. "Where are you planning to go tonight?"

"There is a river to the east, Comrade Major," Vinh explained. "We can go there and find a boat. Then we will go north, up the river. There is a supply shipment point at a bridge where the road crosses the river. There are trucks going both ways there, and we should be able to find transportation."

That sounded reasonable to Yermolav, particularly the part about the boat trip. While he had enjoyed running the Vietnamese into the ground, he wouldn't mind taking a boat the rest of the way.

The Russian got to his feet. "Let's go."

9

Nalan, Laos

Reese's team approached the small Laotian village in a combat patrol formation. They were far too few in numbers to do anything more than run if they made contact with a North Vietnamese unit. But the tracks they were following indicated that the NVA had gone into the village, and they needed to check it out.

Two hundred meters outside the village Reese halted the patrol behind a rice dike for a good look. He saw no sign of uniformed men through the glasses.

"Ski," he said, motioning the sergeant up to his side. "I want you to go around the back and keep an eye on things. If you see anything, fire a round, get the hell outta there and we'll assemble back here."

Kowalski quickly checked his weapon and moved out. Reese watched him through the glasses as he skirted far around the left side of the village and disappeared behind a bamboo wind break. He waited a few more minutes to give him time to get in place before giving the others his order to move out.

They headed off, fingers on their triggers, watching for any sign that the peaceful village was more than it appeared. Santelli felt somewhat exposed as he approached the village, but he saw that children were playing in between the huts, and that was always a good sign. Any time you didn't see children in a village, you could almost bet an ambush was waiting for you. He felt better when he saw them, but he didn't take his finger off the trigger.

As soon as the villagers spotted the team, they hurried out to greet them—another good sign. Soon the Americans were surrounded by dozens of curious Laotians in colorful embroidered clothing. Reese immediately noticed there were no young men of military age in the crowd, but that wasn't unusual for villages in the Cambodian and Laotian border regions. The young men had all been rounded up by the NVA for their work gangs.

The village children were particularly curious about Wilson and swarmed around him. One of the boldest boys touched his dark skin for an instant before pulling back and giggling behind his hands. Wilson was used to this kind of curiosity, particularly from children. Except for black troops of the French and American armies, the natives of southeast Asia had never seen blacks before.

While the villagers studied their new visitors, Santelli and Hotchkiss quickly searched the small houses. "It's clean, Captain," Santelli said. "There's no sign of them here."

"Okay, Whiskey," Reese said to the Nung interpreter. "Let's see what they have to say."

Though the village headman hadn't seen Americans in his part of Laos before, he wasn't reluctant to talk to them. The village didn't have any more food to offer them, and he wasn't sure his two widows would be willing to entertain these strange "long noses" the way they did the North Vietnamese. Therefore, all he could do to secure the safety of the village was to act friendly and talk to them. Hopefully that would be enough.

He talked so much, in fact, that Whiskey had to shut him up to make the translation.

"He say the Cong were here, *Dai Uy*. Maybe two, maybe three hours before."

"How many?" Reese asked. "And where'd they go?"

Again the headman talked animatedly, his hands flying.

"He say maybe fifteen, twenty Cong, and they go to the Xe Ban Foi River," Whiskey translated, pointing to the northeast. "He say they ask him where the boats land and they carry many boxes with them."

"Ask him if they had two Americans with them," Hammer growled.

The headman spoke more hesitantly this time.

"He say the Cong have two long nose prisoners," the Nung reported. "And he think they American. The young one is wounded, but the old one is okay."

"That's them," Hammer said, relieved to hear his men were still alive and that Kegan hadn't been injured by his captors.

"He also say there another long nose with the Cong, but he not a prisoner."

Reese and Hammer exchanged puzzled looks. What the hell was going on here? "Ask him what this other long nose looked like," Reese ordered.

"He say other long nose fat and have yellow hair, cut short like all long noses. He say he wear a uniform with blue up here." Whiskey reached up and touched his lapels and shoulders. "And he carry a pistol."

"The pistol means this guy's an officer," Santelli said.

"The blue collar tabs could be Soviet air force," Hammer added. "They wear light blue as their branch color."

Reese frowned. "What in hell would a Russian flyboy be doing in Laos?"

"Maybe he wanted to take a look at the Spectre," Hammer said. "It fits in with their taking the fire control equipment."

Reese dug into his rucksack and brought out a small, thin book. It looked like a hardcover notebook, but its pages, instead of being paper, were thin sheets of pure gold interlaced with sheets of onion skin. Gold was acceptable currency anywhere in Southeast Asia, and the books were issued to the SOG teams working across the border so that they would have a way to pay the indigenous people for provisions or, as in this case, helpful information.

"How much should I pay this guy?" he asked Whiskey.

The Nung smiled. "He good man, *Dai Uy*. Give him three pieces."

Reese paused. Each page was a half troy ounce of .999 pure gold that would bring at least a hundred and fifty dollars on the black market. "Isn't that a little too much?"

The Nung shrugged. "These good people, *Dai Uy*. They need to buy food because Cong take all their men and they no can work the fields."

Reese didn't care. It wasn't his gold, so he tore out three sheets and handed them to the headman.

The headman's eyes grew wide when he saw his payment. The North Vietnamese never gave him anything; all they did was take. Maybe these Americans weren't as bad as the Communists had said. They hadn't taken any of their food, and now they were paying him for information he would have given them anyway.

Smiling a gap-toothed smile and holding his palms together in front of his face, he bowed low to Reese and rattled off a long string of Laotian.

"He say you are generous man. He say when you come back, he give you a feast for three days. He also say if you want Lao wife, he have beautiful daughter. He say she cherry girl and she want to have tall, rich long nose for husband."

Santelli snickered. "Go for it, Captain. She can be our guide during the day and bunk up with you at night."

Reese smiled. "Tell him I appreciate his offer, but I already have a wife."

"He say no sweat. She be your concubine."

. That got a laugh from everyone, and Reese shook his head slowly. "Come on, guys, let's get outta here while we still have our virtue intact."

The headman was still bowing deeply to Reese when the team moved out.

Even though there was little chance any of the Laotian villagers spoke English, Reese wanted to withdraw from the village before trying to communicate with Hillsboro. As soon as they were far enough away to form a perimeter with good all-round observation, they stopped and Reese got on the radio.

"Hillsboro, Hillsboro," he called the aerial command post and radio relay station, "this is Gray Ghost One One, over."

"Hillsboro, go."

"This is One One. Patch me through to Black Snake. Blue Star priority, over."

"Hillsboro, wait one, out."

A few minutes passed before the radio spoke again. "Gray Ghost, this is Black Snake. Do you have traffic for this station? Over."

"This is Ghost One One," Reese replied. "I need to talk to Black Snake Three."

The Iceman must have been camping out in the CCC radio room, because he came on the air immediately. "This is Black Snake Three, go."

"This is One One," Reese answered. "We've found them. They're two or three hours ahead of us and heading for the Mekong River. Over."

There was a short pause before Snow came back on the air. "Good work, One One."

"The two captured U.S. aircrew are reported to be with them," Reese continued. "And there's another Caucasian traveling with them, as well. From the description we have, Spectre Alpha thinks he's a Russian air force officer who's after the fire control gear. Over."

"This is Snake Three. Copy possible Soviet officers. Has that been confirmed? Over."

"One One, that's a negative. The ID was made based on a description of his uniform as seen by an indig. We have not made visual contact yet. Over."

"Snake Three, roger. What's your status now? Over."

"This is One One. We're going to push on to the river," Reese said, "and try to catch up with them before they can find a boat. Tell the Night Intruders to keep an eye out for river traffic and to blast anything they see."

"Three, roger. Is there anything you need? Over."

Normally Reese did not request or expect an aerial resupply on a cross-border mission. It was too easy for the enemy to zero in on his position when the drop was made. But this wasn't a normal mission. They had come packed for only three days, and this had turned into an open-ended operation. So far they hadn't used up enough ammunition to need resupply, but they would need food in two days, and he might as well have it sent in now.

"One One, roger. I need a packed dry ruck for Spectre Alpha with a full AK ammo load. We can also use some lurps and a couple of donkey dicks if you can get them in to us."

"Snake Three, copy. I'll send them with the recon photos in the morning. Anything further for this station? Over."

"That's a negative. One One, out."

When Reese gave the handset back to Torres and got to his feet, Hammer walked up to him. "I almost hate to ask this question," the flyer said. "But did I overhear you requesting a ration resupply?"

Reese looked puzzled. "We're going to go hungry if I don't. Why?"

"And you asked for donkey dicks?"

Reese laughed. "I knew they wouldn't have any Air Force-issue sirloin steaks and sautéed mushrooms on hand, so I had to order from the Special Forces side of the Army chow menu."

Hammer knew his leg was being pulled, but he wasn't going to ask what donkey dicks were. Whatever they were, if they could eat them, he could, too.

"I'm looking forward to the experience."

Reese grinned. "You'll love it, believe me."

THE MOON CAME OUT, and they were able to make good time through the flatland as they headed for the river. They were still several klicks away when they heard the faint sound of jet engines cruising to the north. A few minutes later they heard muffled explosions in the distance, and the horizon lit up with flashes. Glowing balls raced up from the ground in return as the NVA antiaircraft opened up on their unseen attackers.

"What's going on over there?" Reese asked Hammer.

The major listened carefully to the faint sounds of the aerial attack. "It sounds like the Night Intruders working out, the B-57 Canberras of the Eighth out of Pham Rang. They call themselves the Doom Pussy Squadron, and they work in this area a lot."

"What are they shooting at?"

Hammer shrugged. "It's hard to tell from here. It could be vehicles or maybe a troop concentration. From the triple-A coming back up at them, I'd say it's some kind of troop concentration rather than a convoy. Vehicles usually don't carry that kind of triple-A with them."

The firing died out and the patrol started forward again. A few minutes later they heard jet engines overhead. The sound grew fainter as the plane passed, but then seemed to grow louder again as the faint whine turned into a howling scream.

As it grew louder, Hammer instantly realized what was happening. "Hit the dirt!" he yelled.

The men instantly dropped to the ground, but there was no cover to protect them from whatever was coming. Suddenly the screaming of the jet engines was drowned out with the coughing roar of 20 mm cannons as the diving plane opened up on them. Four lines of 20 mm HE fire flashed down at them, and the shells exploded when they hit the ground, showering dirt and shell splinters all around them.

Reese crawled over to Torres and grabbed the radio handset from him. "Get me Hillsboro!"

The RTO quickly switched frequencies. "Go!"

"Hillsboro! Hillsboro!" Reese shouted into the handset, ducking as more rounds came hammering in. "This is Gray Ghost. We're under fire from friendly aircraft! Check fire! Check fire!"

"This is Hillsboro," came the calm voice over the handset. "Do you know what type of aircraft are making the attack? Over."

"Spectre Alpha says he thinks it's a Canberra!" Reese shouted.

"Roger, One One. I'll get them stopped."

After one more run, the plane pulled up and banked away. The Canberra pilot flicked his running lights on for a brief moment before he flew off to look for another target.

"He says he's sorry," Hammer said as he watched the shadowy shape disappear into the night sky.

"He'd better be fucking sorry," Kowalski growled. "He damn near killed us."

"It's a good thing he only strafed us with his twenties," Hammer said. "If he'd dropped a cluster bomb, he'd have gotten all of us."

"Where did you say those guys are from?"

"They're probably from the Eighth Bomb Squadron in Pham Rang. Why?"

"I want to remember to say thank you the next time I see any of them," the sergeant said. "After, of course, I've punched somebody's fucking lights out first."

"Okay, guys," Reese said quietly. "Coffee break's over. Let's get going again."

"Just a minute, Captain," Wilson called over from where he knelt on the ground. "Hotchkiss is hit."

"Oh, shit!" Reese knelt beside the wounded man. "How bad is it?"

Hotchkiss grimaced. "It's just a scratch."

"He took a piece of shell frag," Wilson said, pulling the two-inch-long shard of jagged steel from the muscles under his left arm. "But I don't think it's too bad. It wasn't moving too fast when it hit." Turning on his red filtered flashlight, the medic quickly examined the wound, cleaned it and bandaged it.

"Can he carry his ruck?" Reese asked.

"I'll pad it so he can."

Hotchkiss got to his feet, and Kowalski helped him into his ruck. The wounded man hefted the pack several times. "It's okay, sir. I can keep going."

"You sure?"

"Yeah."

"Okay, then," the captain said, "let's get going again."

10

Steel Tiger, Laos—July 24

When dawn broke over eastern Laos, the team was awake and getting ready for the day. It had been well after midnight when they finally reached the river, but rather than look for the boat landing, Reese had halted for the night. He had formed the team into a night perimeter and kept at least two men on guard while the others slept.

Though no one had gotten much sleep, Reese knew that a good breakfast would make up for that, so he gave them an hour to get ready before they moved out again. Since they were in open country with good observation all around, Reese let the men light small fires to cook a hot breakfast for a change. In this terrain they didn't have to worry about someone smelling the food cooking as would be the case in the jungle.

Reese was heating a cup of coffee over a small ball of burning C-4 plastic explosive when Torres called him to the radio. "It's the Iceman," the RTO said, handing him the handset.

"Snake Three, this is Ghost One One," Reese answered. "Go ahead."

"This is Snake Three," Major Snow said. "You can expect a package coming your way in about an hour.

Hog Hauler will contact you on your push for delivery instructions, over."

"One One, roger," Reese answered. "We'll be waiting for him. Be advised that we suffered one minor Whiskey India Alpha in that friendly aircraft incident last night, Sierra Foxtrot Charlie Hotel." He spelled out Hotchkiss's rank and first initial of his last name.

"This is Snake Tree, roger. Keep me informed. Out."

With breakfast finished the men rested and checked their equipment while they waited for the aerial delivery.

"Gray Ghost, Gray Ghost," came the voice over the radio handset. "This is Hog Hauler Three Five on your fox mike, over."

"This is Ghost One One Tango," Torres answered, using his RTO's call sign. "Go ahead."

"This is the Hog Hauler," the Herky pilot radioed. "You called and we hauled. I've got a special delivery for you. Where do you want it? Over."

Torres looked around and saw that Reese was talking to the Air Force major. "One One Tango," he replied, "wait one."

"Hey, Captain!" the RTO called out. "It's our resupply bird and he wants to know where to drop it."

Reese unfolded his map as he took the radio handset. "Hog Hauler," he radioed, "this is Ghost One One, over."

"This is the Hog Hauler. I hear you loud and clear."

"This is One One. Try to put our package down at 068374. That's an empty rice field out in the open. You can't miss it."

"Hog Hauler, roger. I copy 068374. Can you put out a marking panel for us to aim at?"

"One One, roger. Wait one."

Torres dug into his rucksack and pulled out two nylon marking panels and handed them to Reese. Cloth rectangles three times as long as they were wide, they were colored international orange on one side, stark white on the other. Reese walked a hundred meters into the field and laid them on the ground in the form of a *T* with the orange side up. The long leg of the *T* was pointing in the direction of the ground winds.

"Hog Hauler, One One Tango," Torres radioed. "The panels are out, over."

"Roger, One One. I've got your orange marker. Stand by for delivery."

The men on the ground heard the sound of aircraft approaching and spotted the C-130 in the distance as she dropped out of the sky. The camouflaged Herky's flaps were down, but her four turboprops were screaming at full throttle as the four-engined transport banked into a final approach. When the pilot lined up on Reese's marker, her rear ramp door opened for the LAPES delivery. The Low-Altitude Parachute Extraction System was the quickest way to get supplies to troops on the ground.

As soon as the plane leveled out a few feet above the ground, the cargo kickers deployed small pilot parachutes out the open rear ramp door. They snapped open in the slipstream and jerked the larger extraction parachute out into the air. The extraction parachute blossomed open immediately, and a small supply pallet came flying out of the rear of the plane. The drop was so low that the pallet didn't even have time to oscillate under the parachute before it slammed into the ground in a cloud of dust and dirt and skidded to a stop.

As soon as the pallet was free, the Herky's pilot sucked the control stick back into his belly, pulling the plane's nose up sharply. With her turboprops screaming and her four-bladed props churning the air, the C-130 clawed for altitude.

Hammer smiled when he saw the Herky's sharp pullout and evasive maneuvers. "I'll bet that guy used to fly supplies into Khe Sanh. He's antsy even when there isn't any triple-A shooting at him."

"There it is," the Herky pilot called down to Reese. "One each special delivery package, no postage due. Glad to have been of service. This is the Hog Hauler, heading back to the barn. Remember, you call, we haul. Ya'll take care now, you hear?"

Reese grinned. "This is One One. Thanks Hog Hauler. We'll catch you at the bar. Out."

Kowalski and Whiskey quickly ran out and dragged the resupply pallet back to their camp. Along with the rations and water Reese had requested was a packet of photos, the latest recon run from the Blackbird. For Hammer there was a fully loaded rucksack with an AK-47 ammo load and an Air Force SR-10 survival radio. The radio would allow them direct contact with the Night Intruder aircraft and hopefully prevent another friendly fire incident.

"Here," Reese said, handing the SR-10 to Hammer, "you're our air-ground liaison officer from now on."

Hammer grinned as he stuffed the radio into his pocket.

"And this ruck should have everything you'll need, including ammo for your AK."

Hammer hefted the ruck and was surprised at how heavy it was. Watching Reese's team march along, he had never thought their packs weighed that much.

"Finally," Reese said, "now that you're a fully functioning part of the team, you get your share of a donkey dick."

Reese picked up the end of one of the twelve-foot orange plastic tubes. "There it is, Nails." He grinned. "One each donkey dick full of water. Hold your canteen out."

Hammer did have to agree that the water container did look somewhat like a giant donkey's tool in a Tiajuana dirty movie. He was going to have to learn that since he was a blue suiter and not a member of their exclusive club, these guys really enjoyed pulling his leg.

The men quickly topped off their canteens and drank their fill from what was left in the tubes. The rest of the water was used for a quick washup. While the rations were quickly broken down and packed into the team's rucks, Reese and Hammer went over the recon photos, looking for anything that might give them a clue as to where the NVA had gone. They knew they had fled toward North Vietnam, and the map showed a bridge site where the river made a big bend eastward several miles to the north.

Checking the photos of that area, Reese saw there had been what looked like a truck park on the eastern side of the bridge, closest to North Vietnam. The site was smoking rubble now. "According to these photos," Reese said, "it looks like your guys really took good care of this bridge site last night."

The photos had been taken when the smoke from the fires still filled the air over the truck park, but much of the damage was still visible.

"They did a real job on it all right," Hammer said approvingly. "But that guy who dropped in on us last night must have had some of his 20 mm ammo left and wanted to use it up before he went home."

"I'm glad that's all he had left," Reese said. "We really don't need that kind of air support."

"What are we going to do this morning?" Hammer asked.

Reese gathered up his map and photos. "Hopefully the air raid took out all of the transportation, but we're going to have to check it out ourselves and see if we can pick up the trail. From the photos and the map it looks like the nearest boat landing is to the north, a little over two klicks. We'll head there first."

VINH'S HEART SANK when the lead boat rounded the bend of the river and he saw his destination—the bridge at the transshipment point on the Ho Chi Minh

Trail. They had cruised down the river all night in these miserable little boats to reach what should have been safety and a place to get a truck to carry their booty north. But what had once been a large, well-camouflaged truck park, a cluster of storage buildings and a ramp leading down from the riverbank was now a smoking ruin. It had been well protected by clusters of antiaircraft artillery batteries, but the B-57 Night Intruders had caught a fuel convoy parked there last night and had bombed it into oblivion.

The extensive camouflage, both living trees and netting, that had covered the facility from aerial observation had been blasted away. What the bombs hadn't destroyed, the exploding fuel trucks had burned to the ground. Smoke still rose from the shattered wreckage of what looked like several dozen Russian tank trucks.

"What the devil has happened here?" Yermolav asked. "I thought you said this area was safe from American bombing?"

"I don't know, Comrade Major," Vinh answered quietly. "It looks like the Yankee air pirates struck here last night."

Yermolav was starting to get tired of hearing Vinh's endless propaganda about the so-called Yankee air pirates. As an officer of the Soviet air force, everything he had seen so far showed him that the American Air Force was doing a very professional, effective job. The fact that they were good at what they did, didn't make them pirates.

In fact, only the most dedicated and professional pilots could press their attacks in the face of the deadly storm of North Vietnamese antiaircraft fire. There wasn't much the Russians could do to make the rag-tag North Vietnamese air force an effective counter to the Americans, but they had given them the greatest concentration of antiaircraft weapons ever seen on any battlefield. This time, however, the Americans seemed to have caught the NVA antiaircraft batteries napping.

As they drew closer to the boat landing, Yermolav could see the twisted barrels and blasted emplacements of dozens of triple-A guns, from the rapid-firing 37 mm and 57 mm multibarrel weapons to the high-reaching, radar-guided 85 mm guns. Not only had the raid taken out the fuel truck convoy, it had also obliterated the site's defenses.

The two boats tied up at the eastern end of the destroyed bridge. Yermolav ordered the fire control equipment and his two prisoners off-loaded while Vinh went to see about finding them transportation. The senior surviving NVA officer was the artillery major in charge of the transshipment point's antiaircraft defenses—or what was left of them.

When Vinh went to him with Yermolav's request for a vehicle, the major exploded. "I don't care what this long-nosed, sweating pig wants," he screamed in Vinh's face. "He's not going to take my last vehicle."

Yermolav walked up in the middle of the major's tirade. He didn't have to understand Vietnamese to know what he had said. His hand went down to the 9 mm Makarov pistol holstered at his belt, but he froze when the NVA troops with the major suddenly aimed their AKs at him. Moving slowly, the Russian let his hand fall to his side, but the AK muzzles didn't waver.

"Tell him I must have it," he hissed at Vinh, barely keeping his temper under control. "Tell him the equipment we carry is essential to the struggle."

Vinh spoke. Again the major screamed back, waving his hands in the air.

"He says," Vinh translated, "that the war supplies moving south are more important to the fight against the Yankees. Because of the attack, he needs every vehicle he can get."

"But I must get this equipment to safety."

Vinh's troops listened to the exchange between the two officers with blank faces. In the North Vietnamese army it was considered unhealthy to overhear command discussions, particularly heated command discussions.

The two American captives listened, as well, even though neither understood a word. Sergeant Kegan knew, however, that the argument wasn't going in favor of the Russian. He, too, had heard the Night Intruder attack last night and recognized what had happened to the truck park.

When the NVA major noticed the two Americans wearing Air Force flight suits, he went berserk. Drawing his pistol, he shouted to his men, and a dozen NVA ran for them, swinging the folding bayonets on their AKs forward to lock onto the muzzles.

"Sarge!" Jones said, his voice rising in panic. "What's happening? What are they going to do?"

Kegan got to his feet and stood in front of his wounded crewman. "Hey you!" he shouted at Yermolav. "Russian! What in hell's going on?"

Yermolav spun around, and when he saw what the major intended, he drew his pistol. Taking him by surprise from behind, he grabbed the Vietnamese officer around the neck and hugged him tightly to his chest. The NVA troops were stunned by this assault on their commander. Most of them kept their AKs trained on Yermolav, but they didn't dare shoot for fear of hitting their leader.

"Tell them to back off!" Yermolav shouted at Vinh, the muzzle of his Makarov pressed tightly against the major's temple.

The Vietnamese officer struggled in Yermolav's grasp, but the bearlike Russian easily held on to him. "You tell this bastard," he snapped, "that if he interferes with this Soviet air force operation one more time, I will personally blow his head off and throw his body in the river for the crocodiles to eat."

Vinh didn't bother to tell the excited Russian there were no crocodiles in Laos, before he translated Yermolav's warning. The NVA major sputtered, but with the cold steel pressed to the side of his head, he had to believe the big long nose would do what he said.

"Tell him he can have the truck," the major spit.

When Vinh translated the reply, Yermolav reached down with his gun hand, took the major's Red Chinese Type 51 Tokarev pistol from its holster and threw it as far as he could before letting the Vietnamese go. Turning his back on the Vietnamese officer, but leaving his pistol in his hand, he walked over to the two Americans and introduced himself.

"I am Major Yuri Yermolav of the Soviet air force," he said in heavily accented English. "Don't worry about them. I will not let them kill you. You are safe with me."

"What happens when you go to sleep?" Kegan muttered. "You can't keep your gun on them all the time."

The Russian laughed. "You will be safe as long as I am alive, Sergeant, and these little men will not dare try to kill me. They are afraid I will come back from the dead and eat them."

Kegan almost smiled at his captor. Whatever the Russian had in mind for him and Jones, at least it wasn't a quick bullet in the head. "We really appreciate your taking care of us, sir."

Yermolav smiled thinly. "It is nothing, American. We civilized men have to stick together in this barbaric country. You are my prisoners and you will be treated properly."

The conversation was broken off by the whining sound of jet engines. Yermolav looked up and saw a flight of F-4 Phantoms diving toward them. He could also see the shapes of loaded bomb racks under their wings, breaking the clean lines of the fighters. The sound of the diving aircraft was interrupted by the coughing roar of triple-A fire as the surviving pair of

57 mm antiaircraft machine cannons opened up on them.

"Take cover!" the Russian yelled.

11

Steel Tiger, Laos

As soon as Reese's team was ready to move out, the cargo parachute, empty rations boxes, donkey dicks and packing materials were quickly piled up and set afire. If any enemy troops were in the surrounding area, they would see the rising smoke plume. But by the time they could investigate, Reese's team would be long gone and all signs of their resupply would be cold ashes.

It took an hour, moving north along the river, before they found traces of the NVA they were tracking. Two and a half klicks north of where they had stopped for the night they came to the boat landing on the west bank of the river. A single Laotian man was fishing on the bank, but his boat was nowhere in sight. He looked up when he saw the Americans but didn't try to run.

"Go see what his story is," Reese told Whiskey as the team took up positions covering the landing.

The Nung quickly came back with the boatman in tow. "He say the Cong take his boat and they go up river, *Dai Uy,*" he reported.

"Does he have another boat we can use?"

"He say he can borrow one from his friend."

"You and Ski go with him," Reese told Santelli. "We don't need him bringing back anything more than a boat."

"Roger that," Santelli said.

While Whiskey and the two Americans went with the boatman, Reese radioed back to Kontoum to inform Snow what they had learned.

"Snake Three, roger," the major answered. "Be advised MACV is becoming very concerned about this situation. They want your assurances that the package can be recovered ASAP. If not, they are prepared to locate it and destroy it from the air. How copy? Over."

Reese almost smiled at that one. If he couldn't locate the North Vietnamese on the ground, how in hell was anyone else going to locate them from the air? But if MACV was that anxious about it, maybe they could turn some of the air assets into an intense aerial recon effort and find those guys for them.

"This is One One. Is higher aware there are two U.S. POWs with that package? Over."

"Snake Three, roger," Snow answered. "They are aware of that, but recovering or destroying the package has the highest priority. It can't be allowed to reach the North intact. Do you copy? Over."

"This is One One. Roger, I understand. Anything further? Over."

"Snake Three, negative. Keep me informed. Out."

Hammer looked grim when Reese told him MACV's attitude about the missing airmen. "I can't fucking believe it,'' he said. ''They're just going to write those guys off.''

''I know,'' Reese said. ''Sometimes you have a hard time knowing who the real enemies are in this goddamn war. But don't worry. We're not going to give up that easily. We'll do everything we can do to get your guys back.''

It took almost an hour before the boatman came back with another boat. A long dugout canoe-type craft with a small motor in the back driving a propeller, it was big enough to carry all of them. The team quickly crowded into the boat, and the boatman pushed away from the dock, heading north, upriver. The unmuffled single-cylinder engine in the rear of the craft chugged and popped as if it was going to die at any moment, but it steadily drove them through the water at a respectable pace.

''If I'd have wanted to join the fucking Navy, I'd have joined the fucking Navy,'' Kowalski mumbled. ''There's no place to hide in this fucking thing.''

Santelli and the sergeant sat in the bow of the narrow boat, carefully scanning the riverbanks as the Laotian boatman kept his craft in the center of the river. The boat would take them where they wanted to go faster than they could go on foot. But, as Kowalski had noted, there was no place to hide in the middle of the river. And, with the motor loudly announcing their presence to anyone within half a mile, they were more than a little conspicuous.

As they cruised along, Whiskey kept up a constant conversation with the boatman, half shouting to be heard over the clatter of the motor. Every few minutes he would turn to Reese and give him a synopsis of what he had learned from the talkative Laotian. "He says 'boo-coo' Pathet Lao on the river this week. He also say many Cong trucks cross over the river at the bridge."

Reese studied his map and the photos, looking to see if there was some way they could approach the bridge without being spotted. The problem was that even with the bombing raid last night the bridge would still be well defended. They were going to have to stop a couple of miles short of the bridge and go the rest of the way on foot.

YERMOLAV LOOKED around at the new damage that had been inflicted on the NVA truck park. The two surviving antiaircraft gun emplacements had been destroyed as had been many of the troops. The NVA major was lying facedown in the red dirt. When two of his men rolled him over onto his back, Yermolav saw that his chest had been torn open by flying debris or bomb fragments. His death was no great loss, but the truck that was to have taken them to safety was also a shattered wreck.

Fortunately the salvaged Spectre equipment hadn't been damaged and his two American prisoners had also survived. Lieutenant Vinh had survived, as well, but he seemed to be in a state of shock. He had never gone through a bombing raid before and was stunned speechless by the sheer level of violence involved and his complete helplessness to do anything about it.

Yermolav had never been bombed before, either, but he was well aware of the nature of death falling from the sky. His technical specialty was aerial weapons systems, which, of course, was why he was sitting in a bombed-out North Vietnamese truck park in Laos with several hundred pounds of American fire control equipment, two American prisoners and no way to transport them.

It had become obvious to Yermolav that he was going to have to take command of the remainder of this operation. Vinh's nerves were shot.

"See if you can find a radio that still works," the Russian ordered him. "And a map that will tell us how to get to Tron Noi in your country."

Vinh looked puzzled. "Tron Noi? I don't understand, Comrade Major. Why do you want to go there?"

"There is a small airfield at Tron Noi," Yermolav patiently explained. "And they will have a radio I can use to request a helicopter to pick us up."

Vinh still looked puzzled, and the Russian had to resist the strong urge to kick him in the ass to get him going. "Don't stop and think about it, you idiot!" he yelled. "Just do it! I want to be gone from this well-protected truck park of yours before the Americans fly over and shit on it again. Move!"

REESE WAITED under cover until the boat disappeared back down the river. The Laotian boatman had been overwhelmed at the payment Reese had given him, but he didn't stick around longer than necessary. The sound of the motor was still echoing from the riverbanks when Torres handed Reese the radio handset.

"It's Hillsboro, *Dai Uy*."

Reese took the handset and keyed the mike. "This is Ghost One One, go."

"This is Hillsboro. I thought you might like to know that I just sent a flight of Fox Fours in on that truck park we hit with the Iron Cranberries last night. Kind of like a cleanup crew to see if there was anyone we'd missed. Black Joker Lead reports they got one truck, the only one they saw. But he also says there were two riverboats tied up at what was left of the bridge. They blasted both of them for you, as well."

"One One, roger. Thanks for the info. If you run any more strikes in that area, tell them to nail any boats they see north of that bridge. I say again north. Make sure they know we're on the water south of it. Over."

"Wilco, One One. I'll keep you informed if we see anything else. Hillsboro, out."

Reese got out his map and studied the terrain around the destroyed truck park, trying to put himself into the mind of the Russian. He couldn't get a truck and his boats had been sunk, but he still had to get his stolen loot to safety. If the Russian had been an infantryman, Reese would have had less trouble trying to read his mind long-distance. But from what they knew, he was Air Force, and that was a completely different mind-set.

"Nails," Reese called out. "Come over here a minute, will you?"

"What do you need?"

"I need to tap into the blue suit mind-set."

Hammer looked quizzical, and Reese explained. "From what we know the raiding party that salvaged your bird was led by a Soviet air force type. We've also learned he has no access to trucks or boats and is still on foot. The question I have is this—what is he likely to do next and where is he going to do it?"

Hammer thought for a long moment, trying to put himself in the mind of the Russian air force officer. "The one thing you can count on is that, as a flyer, he doesn't read maps the same way you do. Terrain is something he flies over, not crawls through. Therefore, I'd say he's more likely to take a direct route to get where he wants to go rather than skirting around difficult terrain the way you would." He grinned. "Now I happen to know there's an airfield right inside North Vietnam, not more than ten, maybe twelve miles from the Laotian border. Right about here." He tapped the map.

Reese noticed that his map didn't show an airfield there, but that didn't mean anything. Even with a war going on, the printing of new maps to reflect the latest information lagged years behind the intelligence-gathering process.

"It's just an auxiliary airfield," Hammer continued. "But we've been keeping a close eye on it while we try to get permission to bomb it. As with hitting any of their air bases, Johnson's scared shitless that we'll kill a Red Chinese adviser and start World War III, so it's hands-off. But my bet is that's where he'll try to take that stuff. He's trained to think in terms of airplanes, and that's the closest place he can find one.''

Reese studied the map for a moment, looking at the approaches to the airfield. There was a road from the Laotian border that wound through the hills and, if Hammer was right, that was the route the Russian would probably take. To the south of the hills the terrain was flatter and provided a good cross-country avenue of approach. Even though it was a longer route, a small, fast-moving unit could cover the ground fast, get in front of them and be waiting to meet them. Maybe they could pull this thing off yet.

He called for the radio. "Hillsboro, this is Ghost One One. Patch me through to Black Snake."

A minute later Snow came on the air. "This is Black Snake Three. Go ahead."

"This is One One. We're going to change the game plan." Reese quickly filled the Iceman in on Hammer's thoughts about the Russian and what he was likely to do next.

"Snake Three," Snow answered. "Wait one while I check my maps. Out." There was a long pause while the operations officer went over Reese's new plan. He was back on the air in a few minutes. "Ghost One One, Snake Three. Your plan looks like a long shot, but I like it. Go for it. I will clear it with higher for you. Also be advised that we are getting reports of increased Pathet Lao and NVA activity in your AO. We don't know what's stirring them up, but be on the lookout for them. Over."

"One One, we'll be looking for them, out."

Reese quickly brought his team together for a briefing. "Okay," he said. "Here's the story. As you know, we've been chasing after these guys for two days now and we still don't even know if we're actually following them or not. It's hard to follow a trail upriver, so we're going to break it off and try a long shot." He paused. "Instead of wasting time trying to pick their trail up again at the bridge, we're going to go into North Vietnam and wait for them to show up there."

There was a stunned silence.

"Jesus!" Kowalski said softly. Special Forces teams had operated in North Vietnam before, some even going into the outskirts of Hanoi, but there was still a mystique about operating in the enemy's home territory.

Santelli grinned broadly. The man in the recruiting office had said, "Join the Army and see the world," and it looked as if he was right. First it had been South Vietnam, then Cambodia, followed by Laos. Now he was going into North Vietnam, and he had only been in-country some six months. What would be next on his sight-seeing tour—Red China?

Torres simply crossed himself, while Wilson locked his jaws and glanced over at Hotchkiss. The sergeant didn't seem to be adversely affected by his shrapnel wound, but he knew that an infection could show up at any time and put him flat on his back in only hours. If that happened in Laos, they could get a Dust-off in

ASAP to Medevac him. But if he went down in North Vietnam, that was altogether another story.

Hotchkiss, however, didn't seem concerned. Like Santelli, he had always wanted to see sunny North Vietnam. "All right!" he said softly.

Whiskey was expressionless. He had been born in North Vietnam, so it didn't really matter to him one way or the other where they went. As long as he could get a chance to kill a few more Cong and get away safely to do it again, he was satisfied.

"What do you have in mind, *Dai Uy?*" Santelli asked.

"Nails says there's a small airfield here." He pointed it out on the map. "And since there's apparently a Russian air force officer in charge of this operation, Hammer thinks this guy will want to get that equipment to an airplane as fast as he can to fly it out. And this is the closest airfield he can reach to call for a plane." He smiled. "Okay, now here's what we're going to do."

12

CCC Kontoum, RVN

Major Snow went over the notes from his last radio conversation with Reese and studied the map of the area east of the destroyed bridge. He agreed that the Russian would probably try to make for the airfield in North Vietnam and try to get a plane. Reese's plan to cut across country to try to get in front of him made sense. The only problem he could see was that Reese didn't have enough people to ensure his survival if something went sour.

As Snow knew all too well, going into North Vietnam could be tricky. He had sent several Shining Brass recon teams in over the past year and a half with varying results. Sometimes you could march around as if you owned the place and no one even bothered to ask who you were. Other times just sticking your nose across the border would get you into hot water.

There was no way to tell what kind of reception Reese would get. A lot would depend on what support the Russian was getting from the NVA to secure his stolen equipment. Snow also knew that the Soviets and the North Vietnamese were uneasy allies. The Russians were even less sensitive than most Americans to the nuances of Asian culture and thought, and all too often effective cooperation between the two was almost nonexistent. He could hope that was the case this time, but he had to prepare a contingency plan in case it wasn't.

Gathering up his maps and photos, Snow walked down the hall to Lieutenant Colonel Newman's office. As usual the CCC commander was up to his ass in paperwork. Unfortunately, even in SOG's clandestine war, bullshit paperwork was the order of the day, not the exception.

"What's up, Jan?" Newman asked, glad for the break.

Snow spread the map on the colonel's cluttered desk and quickly filled him in on the latest change to the operation. "And, sir," he concluded, "I want to suit up a Hatchet Force team and put them on ramp alert in case Reese runs into trouble and needs to be bailed out."

"That's not a bad idea," Newman commented. "He's really going to be hanging out on this. Who do you want to use?"

"His own men," Snow answered. "I will call his team sergeant and have him come in for a briefing."

"Do that," Newman said. "I'll talk to SOG and get clearance for you."

When Sergeant Pierce showed up at CCC an hour later, he found the major in the operations room. Pierce had worked with Snow before in the early sixties when they were both assigned to the White Star program in northern Laos, training an army of Meo tribesmen for the CIA.

That had been Snow's first chance to hit back at the Communists since he had fled his native Hungary and joined the U.S. Army, so he had been in his element. Pierce had fought Communists before in Korea and had been eager to do it again, so the two had worked well together. Although the White Star operation was supposed to have been only a training mission, they had personally led their Meo troops against the communist Pathet Lao many times. They had made a good team back then, and Pierce looked forward to working with the Iceman again.

Pierce saluted Snow when he walked into the room. "It's good to see you again, sir."

Snow hurried across the room and warmly took Pierce's hand. "It's good to see you, too, Ray. It looks like you have been taking care of yourself. What's this—your third tour?"

"Yes, sir. I've got eight months and a wake-up before I hang up my war suit and go back to the reservation."

Snow smiled. "I'll believe that when I see it. You wouldn't know what to do with yourself if you were a civilian again."

"What's the situation, sir?" Pierce asked. "Is Captain Reese in trouble again?"

"Not yet." Snow suddenly turned all-business. He wasn't known as the Iceman for nothing. "But he is quickly heading into harm's way. I want you to put a Hatchet Force team on standby in case he needs to be bailed out."

The major walked over to the map. "There is a small airfield right inside North Vietnam." He tapped the map. "And Reese is heading there to try to cut off the people who salvaged the classified equipment out of that Spectre. If they run into trouble, I want to have someone ready who I can send in on a moment's notice."

"How many people do you want me to suit up?"

"A Jolly Green full—twenty men. I want you to lead the team yourself."

Pierce smiled tightly. "I wouldn't have it any other way, sir."

"I didn't think you would."

"I'll put a call in back to the camp and have them get ready. When can you send us the lift ships?"

"I will lay on a couple of Slicks to transport them up here for a briefing in an hour. You can draw any extra gear you will need from the supply room."

"I'll get right on it."

As Pierce turned and headed for the radio room, Snow went back to his maps. The hardest part of his being an operations officer was that he had to make decisions that could affect the lives of his teams in the field without his actually being there. If he read a map wrong, or missed seeing something on a recon photo, it could get someone killed.

MAJOR YERMOLAV was leading the march again. This time, though, he wasn't trying to run the North Vietnamese troops into the ground. For one thing, he was starting to tire himself; for another, he had to make sure that the porters carrying the Spectre's equipment and the wounded American could keep up.

Back at the bridge he had estimated it would take them only a day and a half to reach the airfield. But he had failed to read the map properly and hadn't taken the hilly terrain into account. After two hours on the road, it was apparent it was going to take a lot longer to reach safety, maybe a full day longer.

Noticing that the NVA were starting to show the strains of the climb, Yermolav called a rest halt. As the Vietnamese porters carrying the litter squatted by the side of the road, the Russian walked back to where the wounded American lay. The man appeared to be unconscious, and his sergeant was tending him.

"How is your friend?" he asked in stilted English.

Kegan looked worried. "He's running a pretty bad fever. And I can't seem to get it to go down."

"We are going to an airfield," the Russian explained. "And once we are there, I will see he gets proper medical attention."

"Could I get some food for him now?" Kegan asked. "The NVA don't want to feed us."

"Do not worry. I will have food brought to you."

The Russian found Lieutenant Vinh talking to the radio operator. Now that they were away from the blasted bridge, Vinh seemed to have recovered a little. He had lost the haunted look and was talking coherently again, but Yermolav wasn't about to let him take back command of the operation. Vinh had proven he was weak, and if there was anything the Russian distrusted, it was weakness.

"I want my prisoners fed," he told the Vietnamese.

"It is our normal procedure, Comrade Major," Vinh replied, "not to feed prisoners until we get them to a holding area. That way they are too weak to try to escape."

Yermolav rested his hand on his pistol holster. "They are my prisoners, Vinh, not yours, and they will be fed."

Vinh eyes flicked down to the holster. "Yes, Comrade Major."

"And I want the same ration for them as the rest of us had. Not a bite less."

"Yes, Comrade Major, I will see to it myself."

"Do that."

THE TERRAIN east of the river was gently rolling and more densely wooded than the plains they had crossed on the west side. Although they wanted to cover ground as fast as they could, Reese's team had to be more alert and keep their point element well out in front to keep them from running into roving enemy units. It was slower going than their trip from the crash site to the river, but Reese was certain they were still outpacing the Russian.

As he walked, Nails Hammer pulled up alongside him. "I know I said I'd keep up with you guys," the Air Force officer said, wiping his forehead on the sleeve of his flight suit. "And I'm not complaining. But when are you going to stop so we can get some sleep?"

"Actually, Nails, we're going to stop as soon as we can find a good place we can defend. I was on a mission in Cambodia myself when I got pulled out to go on this trip and I really can't remember when I last had a full night's sleep."

"Do you guys always live this way?" Hammer asked. "I mean, we've been on the move for a day and a half straight now and we've hardly had time to stop and take a shit."

Reese smiled. "We bust our ass like this when we have to, but we like to take a break as much as anybody. The problem is, the guys we're after are calling all the shots on this one. They're pushing hard, so we have to push even harder just to try to catch up with them."

"I just hope that Soviet blue suiter is getting as tired of this shit as I am," Hammer muttered.

Reese grinned. "The village headman said he was pretty fat, so maybe he's really suffering."

"I sure the fuck hope so."

Back on drag, Hotchkiss passed the word up that they were being followed. Reese hurried back to his position and saw that an NVA unit was coming up on them fast. He thought, however, that they were moving too fast to be tracking them and must have just stumbled onto the same trail by accident. But if they were being tracked, they didn't have time to break trail without leaving signs where they had gone. The best thing he could do now was duck back into the bush and let them move on past.

Quickly and silently the team took up ambush positions along the east side of the trail and settled back into the bush with their fingers on their triggers. The enemy point man showed up a few minutes later, his AK cradled carelessly in his arms as he hurried along. His khaki uniform was darkened with sweat at the armpits, his pith helmet was pushed back from his forehead and he didn't seem to be paying much attention to the ground in front of him or the bush on either side of the trail.

Obviously this was one NVA who wasn't expecting to find Americans in this particular part of Laos. The main body followed closely on his heels, and they were no more alert than their point man was. Not a single one of them even glanced at the bush on the sides of the trail.

After the main body passed, rather than continue on their way immediately, Reese kept the team under cover. They hadn't seen the drag man come by yet. Minutes passed and still no drag man appeared, and Reese was about to continue when Kowalski signaled the guy was coming down the trail. Through his field glasses, Reese saw a man in a dark khaki uniform walking up the trail with his AK slung over his shoulder.

He stopped by the side of the trail directly in front of Hammer's position and unbuttoned his fly to drain his bladder. Afraid the enemy might see the Air Force officer, or at least see Hammer's tracks leading into the bush, Reese caught Kowalski's eye and, dragging his finger across his throat, signaled him to take the guy out quietly.

Normally Kowalski would have simply shot him in the head with the silenced Ruger Mk.1 he carried in his ruck for occasions like this. But since he hadn't packed the pistol for this mission, he would have to do it the hard way with cold steel.

Reaching up with his right hand, he drew his Ka-Bar knife from the sheath taped upside down on his assault harness. Silently he stepped out of the bush behind the NVA, the Ka-Bar held low in his hand.

The drag man must have sensed something, because he started to turn around, but it was too late. Kowalski's left hand clamped over his mouth and jaw, dragging his head back. The Ka-Bar's broad blade sank into the hollow of the man's neck, severing the jugular vein. The NVA struggled briefly, kicked his feet in the dust and went limp.

Kowalski dropped him and waved for Whiskey to come out as he wiped the knife blade clean on the NVA's shirt and resheathed it. They quickly dragged the man's body back into their ambush position.

Hammer walked over while Kowalski and Whiskey were going through the NVA's pockets and rucksack before hiding the body in the bush. He was surprised to see how little blood had flowed from the stab wound at the base of the man's neck. He didn't know that with that particular method of killing a man, the blood drained down into the victim's chest cavity.

This was a side of the war the Air Force officer had never seen before. He was used to a clean war where he shot at his enemies from several thousand feet in the air. He had never had to see the men he had killed, nor smell their blood. This Special Forces way of killing made the war a little too personal for his tastes and there was nothing clean about it. He could see that the North Vietnamese had emptied his bladder in his death throes, and it smelled as if the man had voided his bowels, as well. This was just a little closer to the enemy than he ever wanted to be.

"He doesn't have anything interesting on him, Captain," Kowalski said, handing Reese a thin dark green passportlike book with a furled banner and star insignia stamped in gold paint on the front. "Just his paybook and a couple of family photos."

Reese put the paybook in his ruck. The intelligence specialists back at CCC would translate it later and see what they could get from it. "Cover him up. And get ready to move out."

"Won't his buddies miss him," Hammer asked, "and come looking for him?"

Reese shook his head. "Probably not until they stop for a break. Unlike us, they let their drag men hang quite a way back from the main body, sometimes ten or fifteen minutes' walk. They won't know he's gone until he doesn't show up, and then they won't know when he got lost. Unless they stop for a break in the next fifteen minutes or so, they won't track him back here. And, anyway, we're going to be long gone if they do decide to come back. I'm sorry, but it's going to be a little longer now before we get to take our rest break."

13

Steel Tiger, Laos

Everyone's weariness had vanished in the close encounter with the enemy patrol. Even Hammer had found his second wind as they moved quickly out of the area. Adrenaline racing through a man's blood did that, but Reese also knew that when they came down from the surge, they would be even more tired than before. Adrenaline prepared the body to fight, but there was always a price that had to be paid when the danger passed. Particularly when men were as short of sleep and food as they were.

They pressed on for another hour until they came to a small wooded knoll standing alone in a wide clearing. The position offered good observation of the surrounding area while providing decent cover. Reese passed the word up to the point to make for it.

"We're going to break here for about four hours," he announced when they reached the shade of the trees. "We'll move out again when it gets a little cooler."

Hammer dropped to the ground where he stood and shrugged out of his pack. With the weight suddenly gone from his back he felt a hundred pounds lighter. Leaning the ruck against a small tree, he lay back against it, his legs stuck out in front of him, and took a deep breath. "Jesus," he whispered softly.

Reaching around behind him, he took out one of his canteens. After downing a couple of salt tabs, he drank deeply. Pouring a little water onto his hand, he washed the sweat from his face. He hated to admit it, but he was completely on his last legs. Too exhausted even to eat, he settled back against his pack and was asleep in seconds.

The others took the time to eat a quick meal before they, too, went to sleep. Before the team settled in Reese put one man on guard on each side of their small perimeter. By changing the guards every hour, each of the men would be able to get three hours' rest. It wasn't much, but it should be enough to carry them through until they could stop somewhere for the night.

Choosing to take the last shift on guard, Reese lay back against his own rucksack. Pulling his bush hat down over his eyes, he fell asleep instantly.

Reese awoke abruptly when Santelli touched his shoulder.

"We've got company coming, *Dai Uy*."

A quick glance at his watch showed him that he had only been asleep for a little over an hour. Grabbing his weapon as he rose, he followed the lieutenant to the edge of the knoll. Kowalski was on his belly, watching the enemy unit through Reese's field glasses. Opening and closing his hand, the sergeant flashed five fingers three times. Fifteen men were coming out of the tree line toward them from across the clearing. Obviously they also thought the small wooded knoll would make a good spot to take a break from the hot afternoon sun.

Reese cursed himself for screwing up like this. He was the one who had picked this position and, had he chosen someplace a little less inviting, this wouldn't have happened. There was nothing to do about it now, however, but to stand and shoot it out. If they tried to make a run for it now, they'd be spotted for sure.

"Get 'em on their feet," he whispered to Santelli. "We've got to take 'em out."

Santelli woke the rest of the team, and they hurried to take positions well back from the edge of the trees. Since they didn't have any M-60 machine guns or M-79 grenade launchers, it was going to be a close-in fight—hand-grenade-range close. And that meant they had to let the enemy get right up on them before firing.

That was both good and bad. Up close their initial shots would be more accurate and they would make sure kills. But the close range would also work in the enemy's favor, as well. Their return fire would also be more accurate.

Numerically the odds were against them, but they had three advantages, two small and one big, going for them. First, they had the advantage of a better position and the element of surprise. Those were small things and would change the instant the first shot was fired. But when your ass was on the line even the small shit counted.

Their biggest advantage was that the enemy was approaching from the east and had the sun in their eyes. That would keep them from seeing clearly into the shadows of the trees. Combined with the element of surprise, it might just be enough to tip the scales in their favor.

Hammer knelt behind a tree trunk where Santelli had placed him, his heart hammering. His mouth felt dry, but he could feel the sweat break out all over him. He knew he was on the verge of panicking and tried hard to control his breathing. He checked the position of the selector switch on his assault rifle three times and the magazine lock at least twice.

Santelli had told him to hold his fire until the rest of them opened up first. His trigger finger ached from the tension of holding back. He released the AK's pistol grip and flexed his hand a couple of times, willing his fingers to relax, but it didn't do any good. He slipped his finger back inside the trigger guard.

Slowly the enemy patrol came closer to the knoll, and he counted over a dozen of them walking through the tall grass. They wore light olive uniforms, floppy hats and carried AK-47s at the ready. When the point man was so close that he could almost see the sweat on his face, Hammer had to fight down the urge to scream, shoot or vomit, anything to release the tension.

Crouching in the bush to the right of the Air Force officer, Santelli patiently waited as the enemy point man approached. Like Hammer, he, too, was on an adrenaline high, but he had it well under control and was using it to fine-tune his combat reflexes. He felt the powerful chemical singing through his veins and welcomed the edge he knew it was giving him. The adrenaline was making his vision sharper, his hearing more acute and his nerves steadier. When it came time for him to go into action, he would move faster and with a deadly smoothness. He would become a killing machine, and he counted on that to get him out of the imminent firefight alive.

When the point man was only ten meters from the trees, Santelli sighted in carefully, squeezed the trigger of his CAR-15 and shot him in the head. Not taking his eyes off his next target, he smoothly flicked the selector switch to full-auto, shifted his aim to the next man in the enemy patrol and blew him away with a short burst.

With Santelli's first shot the entire team opened up all at once, and Hammer quickly followed suit with a long burst. The initial burst of fire blew away some half dozen of the enemy patrol. Totally surprised, the others dropped into the tall grass and immediately returned fire.

Now that the shooting had finally started Hammer was surprised to see how cool he felt under fire for the first time. Using the three-round bursts he had mentioned to Reese, he calmly chose his targets, got a good sight picture and carefully squeezed off on them. About half of the time it looked as if he was right on target. All that time he had spent on the firing range was paying off.

When his AK's bolt locked back on an empty magazine, Hammer bent to change magazines. When he came back up, a burst of AK fire splattered dirt in his face. Dropping flat, he rolled to the side to find a better firing position. Jesus! Maybe this ground combat wasn't exactly the piece of cake he thought it was.

Even though the sudden ambush had cut down several of the enemy, Reese's team was still outnumbered, and the enemy continued to put out a deadly storm of return fire. They had to keep the enemy's heads down to prevent them from recovering enough to lay down a base of fire and maneuver against them. In an ambush situation the side that gained and kept fire superiority usually won.

Hotchkiss sprang up from his position and lobbed a grenade far out in front of him. The grenade exploded, sending killing shrapnel out in a five-meter circle. Someone screamed, and Hotchkiss sent a burst of 5.56 mm into the same area, cutting off the scream.

"On the left!" Kowalski suddenly shouted.

Reese spun around and saw two of the enemy trying to sneak around to their flank. Ripping off a long burst, he saw one of the men go down. Kowalski got the other one as he turned and tried to run.

Seeing their flanking attack fail, the remaining enemy tried to run for safety across the clearing. This was what Reese had been waiting for. He got to his feet and sent a burst into the back of a man twenty meters in front of him. "Don't let them get away!" he yelled.

The team opened up with everything they had, burning through magazines as fast as they could. The last man to go down had only made it a dozen meters before he went over on his face.

"Cease fire!" Reese shouted.

The last shots echoed away. Santelli was getting up when he glanced over to where he had last seen Hotchkiss. He didn't see him and moved toward his position. Through the bush he saw the sergeant kneeling on the ground, his hand pressed to his side. Blood was seeping between his fingers.

"Wilson!" he called out. "Over here. Vic's been hit!"

The medic arrived as the sergeant was struggling to get up. "Lie down," he said. "And let me take a look at that."

"It's nothing," Hotchkiss grunted.

Wilson gently pushed the sergeant's hands away so he could look at the wound. "Unbutton your shirt."

The bullet had torn a jagged furrow through the thin layer of muscle over Hotchkiss's ribs, but didn't seem to have entered his body.

"How bad is it?" Reese asked.

"I think he's only got a broken rib," Wilson said as he carefully cleaned the wound and gently probed the jagged rent in the skin. "It doesn't look like the bullet went on into his guts."

"You're sure as hell pushing the three-heart rule, Vic," Reese said.

There was a Department of Defense policy that said when a man received his third Purple Heart for wounds sustained in combat his tour was considered to be completed and he could be sent back to the States.

Hotchkiss grinned as Wilson carefully bandaged the wound, then taped his side to give support to the broken rib. "I'm not trying to get sent home, Captain. I just want to spend a week in Nha Trang."

Reese grinned. Everyone wanted to spend a week in Nha Trang, himself included. Along with being home to the Fifth Group Special Forces Operational Base, the headquarters for all SF in-country, Nha Trang was a world-class resort town with blinding white beaches and rolling surf coming in off the bay. It also had some of the best-looking bar girls and classiest cat-houses in all of Southeast Asia.

"You've got it, Sarge," he told Hotchkiss. "A week's in-country R and R at SFOB as soon as we get back. I'll cut orders sending you down there to do a survey of the bars and cathouses."

Hotchkiss grinned even wider. "I'll hold you to that promise, sir."

Wilson dug into his aid bag and came out with a small bottle of green pills and handed them to Hotch-kiss. "Take two of these three times a day."

Hotchkiss immediately recognized the pills as tetracycline, the powerful, broad-spectrum, cure-all antibiotic of the war. Anything from the clap to gun-shot wounds was treated with tetracycline. He took two of the bitter-tasting pills and washed them down with a swallow of water.

While Wilson and Reese tended to Hotchkiss, Santelli and the others made a quick search of the clearing for anyone who might have survived the savage firefight. Whiskey found one of the enemy still alive, leaving a blood trail as he crawled away through the grass. Without even thinking the Nung drew a bead on the back of his head and blew his brains out. On a mission like this one, they didn't have time to screw around with prisoners.

Only after the man was dead did he realize that maybe he should have talked to him before killing him. He shrugged and moved on. Maybe he'd try talking first to the next one he found if he found any more alive.

As before, the enemy bodies and their packs contained little of interest except for paybooks and a few letters from home. Whiskey found several cans of herring packed in Red China, which he added to his own rations, and Kowalski picked out two hundred rounds of Chicom 7.62 mm ammunition still in their fifty-round factory paper wrappings.

"You might need this," he said, offering the ammunition to Hammer.

"Is it safe to use?" the Air Force officer asked. "We got a MACV bulletin recently warning us not to use captured enemy ammunition."

Kowalski smiled knowingly. "That's because of the Operation Eldest Son stuff. Some of the road runner teams have been running around planting booby-trapped enemy ammunition in NVA supply caches, but you won't find any of that stuff this far north."

"You guys do a lot of that kind of thing, don't you?"

Kowalski grinned broadly. "Every chance we get. Anything we can do to fuck with their minds makes our job just that much easier."

After completing his check of the bodies, Santelli walked up to Reese with several soldiers'. identification books. "Hey, Dai Uy," he said, holding out one of the books, "I think these guys are Laotian. Pathet Lao."

Reese saw the cursive, Sanskrit-style writing on the cover and agreed. "That sure as hell isn't Vietnamese. Did they have a radio with them?"

Santelli shook his head. "Nope."

Reese was relieved. The lack of a radio probably meant the enemy patrol had been simply moving to a new location and hadn't been actively looking for them. That would indicate they had probably still not been spotted and therefore still had a good chance of pulling this off. He also knew that the closer they got to North Vietnam the greater the chance they had of running into more patrols. They still had to move fast and continue to stay alert.

"Okay," Reese growled, "let's grab our stuff and get the hell outta here before someone shows up to see what all the noise was about."

Leaving the enemy dead where they had fallen, the team moved to the northeast. As soon as they had moved a klick away from the ambush site, Reese found another good location and called a halt again. Since their last rest period had been so rudely interrupted, he kept half of his men on guard this time while he made a radio call back to Kontoum. Now that they had finally made contact and had possibly compromised the mission, CCC needed to know.

The Hillsboro radio operator quickly patched him through to Major Snow. "This is Black Snake Three. Do you have traffic for this station? Over."

"This is Ghost One One, roger," Reese answered. "Be advised that we've made contact with a roving patrol of Pathet Lao. We got them all, but we had to break away to the north to evade. We'll be stopping here for a rest break and moving out again later this evening. Our Echo Tango Alpha at the objective is midmorning tomorrow. Over."

"Three roger. Keep me informed. Out."

14

Steel Tiger, Laos

Reese had just closed his eyes and leaned back against his rucksack for a short nap when Torres hurried up to him. *"Dai Uy,"* he said, holding out the radio handset, "it's Snake Three again."

Reese frowned as he took the handset. What had the Iceman forgotten to tell him? "This is One One. Go ahead."

"This is Black Snake Three," the major radioed. "Request authentication, over."

Now Reese was really puzzled. What in hell was going on? Why was Snow requesting authentication? The only time that was done was when there was some question about who you were talking to. Reese recognized Snow's slight European accent and was sure the major recognized his voice, as well. Whatever it was, though, he had to go through the drill because Snow had requested it.

Flipping back to the authentication code page in his SSI, he chose a two-letter code group. "This is Gray Ghost One One," he radioed back using his full call sign in case the radio message was being recorded. "Authenticate Bravo Lima, over."

There was a short pause as Snow worked out the proper two-letter coded response from his own SSI. "This is Black Snake Three. I authenticate Delta Foxtrot, over."

Reese checked his list and saw that the response was correct. "This is Ghost One One. Roger, Delta Foxtrot, authentication correct. Go ahead."

"This is Black Snake Three. Be advised there has been a change in your mission plan. Higher denies permission for you to go on to your final objective. If you cannot recover the package before crossing over into North Vietnam, you are to effect immediate mission closure. Do you roger, over?"

Reese was stunned. What had happened to the urgent priority on the classified Spectre fire control gear? "This is One One," he radioed back. "What about the U.S. personnel accompanying the package? Over."

"Snake Three, they are to be written off, too. Do you roger? Over."

"One One, I copy," Reese said slowly, not believing what he was hearing. "The captured U.S. personnel are to be abandoned. Over."

"Black Snake Three. That's affirmative. Negative further. Out."

Reese gave the radio handset back to Torres. If he hadn't known better, he would have thought that Colonel Marshall, who had recently been sent DEROS, had returned to Saigon and was running the MACV-SOG operations shop again. This was the kind of shit the colonel pulled all the time, but he knew Marshall was long gone to his reward of a cushy desk job in the Pentagon. The SOG operations shop was supposedly in the hands of a real soldier for a change, not a ticket puncher, but obviously some things hadn't changed.

He had no idea what had gone wrong this time. Whatever it was, he was going to have to find a way around it. He had never left a captive American behind if there was any way to get him back. Even though the captives weren't SF, they were Americans, and that was enough. Also, Hammer was never going to agree to leave his people behind. He looked over and, catching Hammer's eye, motioned to him.

"We've got us a problem here," he told the Air Force officer. "My operations officer has just informed me that we are not to cross over into North Vietnam under any circumstances."

Hammer's face hardened and he shook his head slightly. "Why the fuck would they tell you something like that?"

Reese shrugged. "I don't know. But it stinks of pure politics to me. My bet is that someone in the Pentagon leaked word of this operation to the White House and our President has gotten personally involved. Or we may be stepping on the Company's toes again."

When he saw the blank look on Hammer's face, Reese explained. "This is not the first time something like this has happened. The White House tries to run our war long-distance the same way it tries to control the air war you guys fight. Also this may have CIA input. I've been ordered to close missions before because we were getting in the way of some ongoing CIA operation. It's the old story of the right hand not knowing what the left is doing. It happens to us all the time.''

"But what are we going to do?" Hammer's frustration was evident in his voice. "We can't just leave Kegan and Jones in the hands of the NVA. Jones won't make it in a prison camp. He's wounded pretty bad.''

"I know." Reese shook his head. "If I'd had any idea this was coming, I would have faked a radio problem or something so I wouldn't have received the order. As it is now, with the proper authentication and all, if we cross the border, we're all going to get our asses courtmartialed when we get back.''

"So what are you going to do?" Hammer repeated.

Reese grinned. "We're going to go on across, anyway. But first we'll have to go through a little drill that we call CYA in the Army.''

Hammer smiled back. "We call it the same thing in the Air Force. Cover Your Ass.''

Reese quickly called the team together and explained what Snow had said and what he wanted them to do about it. Broad grins broke out on all of their faces. If there was anything they liked to do, it was sticking it up the asses of the chairborne warriors back in Saigon.

Santelli laughed. "All right!"

"Those assholes," Kowalski growled.

Reese grinned. "Okay, guys, let's do it and make it sound real. But remember, only use two mags.''

The team encircled Reese and held their weapons at the ready. The captain raised his hand theatrically. "Three, two, one, fire!"

Reese keyed the mike as soon as the men started shooting. "Hillsboro, Hillsboro, this is Ghost One One," he shouted over the roar of the small-arms fire. "Patch me through to Black Snake. Over."

"Hillsboro, wait one."

"This is Black Snake," the radio operator at Kontoum answered. "Go ahead."

"This is Ghost One One. Advise Snake Three we're under heavy attack."

Reese paused and held the transmission switch down to let the firing be heard over the radio. The characteristic sound of Hammer's AK added greatly to the sound of a real battle. Someone threw a grenade, and the explosion punctuated the automatic fire nicely.

"We are withdrawing to the east at this time to try to break contact. Over."

"This is Black Snake." The Kontoum radio operator's voice sounded worried. "Can you hold for Snake Three? Over."

"That's a negative!" Reese shouted. "We've got to get out of here now!"

"Ghost One One!" the RTO called, trying to restore the communication. "Come in, please! Ghost One One!"

"Cease fire!" Reese shouted as he gave the headset back to Torres.

Everyone was wearing a big grin as they replaced the expended magazines in their weapons.

Reese chuckled. "Okay. That's taken care of. Now let's get the hell outta here."

"Where?" Hammer asked.

"Like I told the man—" he pointed toward North Vietnam "—east."

Hammer smiled grimly. He liked the way these Special Forces people thought.

Now that the team was somewhat rested again Reese pushed on. They were still several klicks from the North Vietnamese border, and he wanted to cross before they stopped for the night.

MAJOR SNOW SMILED thinly as he listened to the recording of Reese's radio call. He immediately recognized what Reese was doing. In the grand tradition of Special Forces operations the commander on the ground was telling the desk jockeys in Saigon that they had their heads stuck up their asses and obviously didn't recognize the seriousness of the situation. He was also divorcing himself from the politics of the mission and was focusing on the only thing that really mattered—the lives of the American prisoners.

Politicians and planners had the luxury of worrying about the sanctity of national boundaries and other diplomatic bullshit. To the man in the field the only thing that had any meaning was the lives of his comrades. Although the prisoners weren't SF, they were American and they were being held captive by the enemy. If there was any way they could prevent it, the Special Forces didn't leave POWs behind.

The major had to admit that the staged firefight had sounded very authentic. Reese had had the right note of panic in his voice and had sounded like a man with a real problem. Even though Snow could hear there was only one AK in the roar of automatic weapons fire, he knew no one at MACV would be able to detect that. Reese was covering his ass well, and Snow hoped he could pull it off without getting caught. If he recovered the POWs alive, it wouldn't matter how or where he had done it; he'd be a hero. If he failed to get them out, the assholes at MACV would throw him to the wolves.

There was almost nothing Snow could do from Kontoum to help him. Maybe it was time he got Sergeant Pierce and his men involved. Reaching across his desk, he picked up the phone and dialed the isolation building on the compound.

"Isolation, Sergeant Pierce," the voice on the other end of the line said.

"This is Major Snow. How about coming over for a minute? I need to talk to you."

"On the way, sir."

When Pierce arrived, Snow quickly filled him in on what had happened. The team sergeant was as outraged as Snow had been. "What in hell are we going to do now, sir? We can't just leave those guys over there."

Snow smiled thinly as his eyes went to Pierce's master blaster wings on the left breast pocket flaps on his fatigues, his senior parachutist's badge. "We're not. How many of your men are jump-qualified?"

Pierce grinned. As he had predicted, working for the Iceman was proving to be interesting. "Most of them are, sir. If we do a low-level static line jump, all of them can make the drop."

Snow nodded. That was exactly the answer he had expected. Many of the Nung CIDG troops had been airborne-trained at the SF in-country jump school at Bon Son, particularly the Mike Force strikers found in Reese's A-410. But, as Pierce had said, the non-jump-trained Nungs would survive a low-level static line jump even if someone simply suited them up and and kicked them out the door.

"Good," Snow said. "Go draw your jump gear from supply and run your people through a few practice PLFs."

Pierce smiled. A good PLF, a Parachute Landing Fall, was the key to a man surviving a parachute landing without breaking something. On a low-level static line jump the trip down was brief, very brief. The jumpers would barely clear the door before their static lines would pull the parachutes open. Then, seconds after the shock of the parachutes deploying, they would be on the ground. There would be no time for a man to worry about the wisdom of jumping out of a perfectly good airplane. Either it would work right or he would be dead before he had time to realize that something had gone wrong. But, dead or alive, a parachute drop was still the fastest way to get troops on the ground in a hurry.

"What will we be jumping from, sir?"

"I don't know yet, but I'm going to try to get you a Herky."

"With the unqualified men I've got," Pierce said, "that would probably be best. I can kick their asses off the rear ramp before they even know they're gone."

Snow smiled knowingly. The jumpmaster had had to kick him out the door of a C-47 on his first jump. After that first time, though, he had been more than willing to throw his body into empty space every chance he could get. He knew that if the Nungs survived the jump, they would brag to their friends about it afterward.

As THE SUN WENT DOWN over the hills, Major Yermolav called a halt. From what he could tell from the map they had made it almost halfway to the airfield. If they got an early start in the morning, they should reach their destination by late afternoon. Then, if they could get a plane to the airstrip early enough the next morning, he would be back in Hanoi by noon.

It wouldn't come a minute too soon for him. He had enjoyed just about all of Southeast Asia he could stand. His gut was still rumbling a little, but he hadn't had to stop by the side of the trail more than three or four times all day. All he needed now was a bottle of vodka and a real Russian meal and he would be back to normal.

After, of course, he took a long, hot bath. It had been so long since he had bathed that he could smell himself, and he didn't like what he smelled. He had smelled day-old corpses that weren't half so rank. He didn't understand how any infantryman, Russian or Vietnamese, could live with the stench from their crotches and armpits.

Lieutenant Vinh hurried up to him with his radio operator in tow. "Comrade Major," the Vietnamese said, "one of our ground units has reported firing south of us earlier this afternoon. They don't know what caused it, but they think the Yankees may have infiltrated a combat team into the area."

"Why would they have done that?"

Vinh almost sneered at the Russian's naïveté. He might be an aviation expert, but he had a lot to learn about ground operations and the way the Americans operated. If the Yankees knew the two American flyers had been captured, they would do anything they could to try to recover them. He was constantly amazed at the effort and lives they would expend trying to recover downed flyers or their wounded from a battlefield. In the North Vietnamese army a prisoner or a wounded man was of no further use and was forgotten.

"It could be a routine reconnaissance, Comrade," he said. "But I think they are looking for us and your two Yankee prisoners. Also I am sure they want to get the salvaged equipment back."

"How far to the south are they?"

Vinh checked his map. "At least fifteen kilometers, maybe more."

"Show me on the map."

When Yermolav saw where the firing had been reported, he relaxed. Whoever had been involved, they were much too far away to have anything to do with him. If a Yankee unit was following him, it would be coming up behind him from the west, not wandering around fifteen kilometers to the south. That was half a day's march away, if not more.

"Don't worry about them," Yermolav said, dismissing the threat. "Tell your men we are staying here for the night. But tell them not to light fires to cook. I am tired and I don't want the Yankee pilots interrupting my sleep tonight."

"Yes, Comrade Major."

"Also, see that my prisoners are properly fed. I don't want them to die before I get them to Hanoi."

"Yes, Comrade Major."

Following his orders to the letter, Vinh ladled out two small bowls of cold rice and picked up a tin of the canned herring provided by the People's Republic of China. This was exactly what his men were eating tonight, and it would have to do for the American prisoners. He still questioned the wisdom of feeding prisoners, but he wasn't about to risk the Russian's temper. Yermolav had proved to be as crazy as all the other Russians he had known.

Sergeant Kegan silently took the bowls and herring tin from the Vietnamese officer. Helping Jones sit up, he fed him one of the bowls of rice and most of the herring. The wounded airman's fever had gone down, but he was still weak, barely able to eat. After giving him a drink of water, the sergeant washed the sweat from his face and helped him get comfortable for the night. Hopefully Jones would make it through the night, through tomorrow's march to the airfield, to the medical attention the Russian officer had promised. Until then there was nothing Kegan could do but wait.

15

North Vietnam—July 25

Shortly after midnight Reese's team crossed the border into North Vietnam and, as soon as he found a well-hidden spot, Reese called a halt for the night. The exhausted men wasted no time finding a comfortable place to sleep. Even those standing their turn on guard had a difficult time staying awake.

By first light that morning they were on the move again for the final leg of their march to the airfield at Tron Noi. The night's rest had done everyone good, and they made quick time through the scattered bush and low trees. Because he had no way of knowing how far the Russian had come through the mountain route, Reese knew they had to cover ground fast to arrive at the airfield first. The closer they got to their objective the more careful they would have to be.

Reese kept the point man well out in front, but they encountered no one, nor any sign that anyone had moved through the area recently. It was almost as if they were alone in their own little corner of Southeast Asia, but that didn't ease his mind. The recon photos he had been sent didn't cover the area around the airfield, so he had no way of knowing what kind of garrison or defenses it had. Without that information he would have to wait until he saw the place before making his attack plan.

He didn't like to have to shoot from the hip that way, but he really didn't have any other choice. If MACV headquarters hadn't turned their backs on him, he could have requested another Blackbird photo run over the area. But breaking his radio silence to request that now would only let them know he was continuing his mission against orders. MACV would simply order him again to break off the mission and return ASAP. And Reese would never do that, not while there was any chance of getting those two airmen back alive.

He had his ass on the line as it was, but at least he had an almost plausible cover story. If he was successful and got both the prisoners and the captured equipment back, MACV would turn a blind eye to his having disobeyed the order to stay out of North Vietnam. But if he failed, or if he got back in contact with them before he was successful, his military career would be finished.

Reese was a Regular Army officer, but not a career soldier in the usual sense of the term. As far as he was concerned, he was in the U.S. Special Forces, not the U.S. Army. In his mind the two organizations were worlds apart. As long as he could stay in the Special Forces, he would stay in the Army. And, with the war going on, that meant he wanted to be stationed in Vietnam.

He had gone home after his first tour was over, but between fighting with his wife and finding himself a stranger in his own country, he had volunteered to come back to Vietnam early. Even with the difficulties he was in now, though, he knew his decision to return to the war had been the best thing he could have done. Regardless of all the assholes in high places who made self-serving, meddling decisions designed to advance their own careers rather than defeat the Communists, the war was still the only thing that made any sense to him.

He knew that if he stayed in-country long enough, though, he would be pulled out of the field and put into a staff position somewhere. But Special Forces staff work was at least still Special Forces, and he could continue to be a real part of the war. If he had one of the do-nothing, ticket-punching, ass-kissing, political staff jobs that non-Special Forces officers had to endure, he would resign his commission.

Once more his future was dependent on the politics of his present mission, not the military considerations. He had made his decision and would play it out to the end. If he got thrown out of the Army for doing what he felt was right, so be it; he would become a mercenary. There was more than one army that would gladly hire the well-honed skills of a Special Forces Vietnam combat veteran.

EARLY THAT MORNING Major Snow and Sergeant Pierce sat in the radio room at the CCC headquarters in Kontoum drinking coffee and listening to the radios. They really didn't expect Reese to try to contact them unless he ran into trouble, but old habits were hard to break.

"What kind of guy is this Reese?" Snow asked.

"He's pretty straight, sir, and a good officer," Pierce answered as he poured himself another cup of coffee from the pot on top of the filing cabinet. "But he's a little hardheaded when he thinks he's right. Also, he's got a real low bullshit tolerance level. He hadn't been with the team two weeks before he went head-to-head with Colonel Marshall over a fucked-up Cambodian mission."

"This was before Marshall picked your team to work with SOG, right?"

Pierce nodded. "Reese thinks we got assigned to Hatchet Force duties as a punishment because he'd pissed Marshall off so badly."

"That sounds like something Marshall would do all right," Snow replied. "He was famous for that sort of vindictive shit. He never did understand the concept that the SF is an all-volunteer organization and that SOG is even more so. Your team could have gotten out of that assignment because you hadn't volunteered for it. All you would have had to do was go to Fifth Group."

"We knew that, sir," Pierce said. "But we wanted to stay together as a team." He flashed a quick grin. "Also, we figured that working for SOG might be more interesting than the routine shit we were doing down in the Delta."

Snow laughed. "At least no one could say this mission is routine."

"You've got that shit right, sir."

"Speaking of routine," Snow said, "what do you think Reese is doing now?"

Pierce thought for a moment. "For one thing, sir, since he's been maintaining radio listening silence so you can't contact him and order him to turn around, I'd say he's still driving on to that little airfield. Whatever else happens, my feeling is that he's not about to leave those two Air Force guys behind if there's any chance at all that he can get them back."

"How do you think he'll try to do that?"

Pierce tapped the symbols on the map showing the North Vietnamese airfield. "Considering how few people he's got with him, he'll probably try to ambush the Dinks here after they get within sight of the airstrip. They'll feel safer then and will probably be slacking off a little."

"I need to contact him before that," Snow said, "and let him know your men are standing by if he needs help. But since we're being so closely monitored on this mission, I am going to have to use a clear code to talk to him."

"What's that, sir?"

Snow smiled. "It's a technique left over from the resistance days in World War II that you use when you know the enemy is listening to your radio traffic. We used it in the Hungarian Revolution because we only had captured Soviet radio equipment and we knew the Russians were monitoring all our channels."

"How does it work?"

Snow smiled. "Well, you are going to have to tell me as much personal information about him as you can. The more personal the better."

Pierce smiled back. "Well, sir, I don't know all that much about him. We don't go out drinking together or anything like that, but I do know he's got a girlfriend in Saigon."

"Good. What's her name?"

"Laura Winthrop."

THE SUN WAS HIGH when Reese's team finally reached a small knoll half a klick north of the airfield. Even with the sleep they had gotten the night before, they were still operating at a deficit and the push to their objective had tired them out again.

Leaving the others to eat and rest, Reese dropped his ruck and took Hammer and Santelli to the edge of the knoll to scout the area. Keeping well under cover, Reese focused his field glasses on the airfield below, but there was little to see. At one end of the hard-packed laterite airstrip were three frame buildings, a rickety control tower and what looked like a small fuel dump. There was evidently no one walking around, but two bicycles were leaning against one of the smaller buildings.

"Is this field supposed to be in operation?" he asked Hammer.

The Air Force officer held his hand out for the glasses. "All we know is that the MiGs use it to refuel when they run outta gas chasing our guys returning from strike missions."

Hammer brought the glasses up to his eyes and studied the layout. He spotted a pair of radio antenna masts sticking up from the wooden control tower and what he thought was an underground bomb shelter at its base. The one thing he didn't see was a radar antenna, which meant approaching aircraft would have to notify the tower by radio that they were coming.

"It doesn't look like anyone's home," Hammer said as he brought the glasses down.

"They also could be taking their midday siesta," Santelli commented. "Only mad dogs and recon teams go out in the noonday sun."

"And we're the mad dogs, right?" Hammer said.

"You got that shit right, Major."

"If you were running that place down there," Reese asked, "what kind of duty hours would you keep?"

Hammer thought for a moment. "Well, most of our bombing is done during the day—the MiGs usually aren't that good at night interception over the Trail, anyway. So I'd say it's active only during daylight hours, and then only when someone's inbound. The rest of the time they'll be on standby."

"Would you keep a radio watch at night?"

"Sure."

Reese scanned the airstrip again, seeing no sign of movement. "Jack," he said, turning to Santelli, "how'd you and Ski like to sneak in a little closer and see what in hell's going on down there?"

Santelli's grin threatened to split his face. "Sure, why not? I could use the exercise."

SANTELLI CREPT through the bush around the far end of the airfield as stealthily as a hunting tiger. With the sun high there were no shadows to hide in and the dark colors of his tiger stripe jungle camouflage uniform stood out dramatically against the sun-dried vegetation of the plains. He had left Kowalski behind and was making the close-in recon of the buildings alone. That way, if he was spotted, Ski could lay down covering fire for him while he made his escape.

Santelli checked the open ground in front of him—no one in sight. He dashed to the back of the small wood frame hut by the control tower. Dropping down to his belly, he crawled around to one side for a better look. Poking his head around the corner, he saw that the door was propped open and the rain shutters on the windows were tied up for better ventilation. The building didn't look big enough to be a barracks, so he figured it had to be the radio shack.

Keeping low, he moved forward until he could see around the corner of the open door. It was, in fact, the radio shack. Inside, the NVA on radio watch was dozing in his chair, his head back, his eyes closed and a headset covering his ears. Santelli was no radio expert, but it looked as if most of the equipment was the long-range aircraft radio gear he expected to see. The wall behind the radios was decorated with centerfolds from *Playboy* magazines. He recognized several of the ladies from last year's issues and wondered where in hell the enemy was getting them.

There was little else to see, so he crawled to the back wall of the hut and noticed two cables running from the roof over to the rickety control tower. They seemed to connect to two antenna masts that rose high above the thatched roof over the open-sided control room atop the tower.

No weapons or equipment were visible in the tower, no machine guns to protect the approaches to the buildings below. Apparently the North Vietnamese garrison didn't feel threatened, since their little airfield was so far inside their own country. That alone would make the good guys' job considerably easier when it came time to attack the place.

Behind the radio shack was a fairly large, open-sided building with wooden tables and benches at one end—a typical NVA-style mess hall. No one was around, so he went to check it out.

In the fire pits at the end of the mess hall banked coals to cook the evening rice sent a tendril of smoke into the still air. By counting the enameled metal rice bowls stacked on the serving table, Santelli figured there couldn't be more than fifteen men eating at one sitting. Also, there were only three bottles of *nuoc-mam,* the pungent Vietnamese fish sauce; figuring at least five men to a bottle, that confirmed the count of the bowls. It had to be a small garrison.

Right outside the mess hall was a small, carefully tended garden where the North Vietnamese cooks grew vegetables and herbs to supplement their boring rations. Most of the permanent NVA camps he had seen had always had a small garden. At the end of the garden were two banana trees with large clusters of fruit hanging from their branches. Reaching up, Santelli broke off two large, ripe bananas and stuffed them in the side pockets of his fatigue pants.

The building next to the mess hall had to be the sleeping quarters for the garrison. The building was large enough to house anywhere from fifteen to twenty men. He was tempted to poke his head in the door and take a quick look around, but he knew better. The chances were that at least one guy was awake reading a book or whacking off, and he'd be spotted for sure.

Glancing down at his watch, he decided to break off his recon. He had seen enough to draw up an attack plan and he needed to rejoin Kowalski before the sergeant got too antsy about his absence.

16

Tron Noi Airfield

Santelli was munching on a banana when he and Ko-walski arrived back at the knoll. "They're down there all right, Captain," he said, holding up the banana peel. "And they're eating pretty good for Dinks."

"Did you bring me one of those, LT?" Hotchkiss asked.

Santelli dug into the side pocket of his fatigue pants and produced another banana. "Here." He tossed the fruit to the sergeant. "I knew you'd want one."

"What did you find?" Reese asked.

"There are a dozen or so guys down there," San-telli reported. "And it looks like they're North Viet-namese air force REMFs instead of hard-hat NVA." He looked at Hammer and grinned. "Except for the guy on radio watch, everyone else was busy bagging zees. We could walk in there and take the place over without firing a shot."

"What about their weapons?"

"All I saw was a rusty old SKS leaning against the wall in the radio shack. There are no heavy weapons emplacements, but that doesn't mean they don't have an RPG or machine gun tucked away somewhere."

"What do they have for commo?"

"The smallest hut down there is their radio shack, and it's got several large radios. They look like VHF and UHF air control stuff to me, but Torres will have to check them out to make sure."

"Tell 'em about the Playmates, LT," Ski said.

"Oh, yeah." Santelli grinned. "They've got a raggedy-ass collection of *Playboy* centerfolds pinned up on the wall of the radio shack. But it was all last year's stuff or older. No Miss July '68."

"That's too bad," Hammer said. "I've got her up on the wall of my hootch back at Udorn, and I can tell you she's got one of the finest asses in the business."

"That's right," Santelli said enviously. "You guys get your *Playboys* flown in every month direct from the States, don't you?"

Hammer grinned. "That's one of the major benefits of wearing a blue suit."

"Okay, guys," Reese said, "let's get back on the subject. We have an attack to plan. We obviously beat the Russian here so now we have to figure out how we're going to relieve him of his prisoners and that salvaged electronic gear."

"Why don't we just wait for them here?" Santelli asked. "They'll probably be slacking off when they get this close to going home. So, while they're stumbling around with their heads up their asses, we just 'bush them, grab our guys and haul ass outta here."

"I'd like to do exactly that," Reese said. "But it might not be that simple. For one thing, one of the prisoners is wounded and he may not be able to walk. Also, don't forget all that fire control equipment.

That's what they sent us out here to recover in the first place.''

"Can't we just blow it in place and leave it?" Santelli asked.

"We may have to," Reese said, "but first I want at least to try to recover it intact."

"So what do you have in mind?"

"First off," Reese said, "how'd you and Whiskey like to take another little walk?"

"You want us to go up in the hills and run a recon on the Russian, right?"

Reese nodded. "If he's moving as slowly as we think he is, he may not get here till dark. If we're going to be ready for him, I need to know where he is now and when he's going to get here."

Santelli studied the map. "That's going to be a real hump, *Dai Uy*. He could be fifteen miles away, and I don't have a radio to call back to you."

"You think you're up to it?"

"No sweat. We'll just run it in relays. Run an hour, walk ten minutes. We can cover ground pretty fast that way, but we won't get back till almost dark."

Torres was listening to the radio with a puzzled look on his face. "Captain, I'm getting some real strange stuff coming in over the radio."

"What kind of strange stuff?"

"They're transmitting in the clear," he said, holding out the radio handset. "But I think it's some weird kind of code. Listen."

Reese took the handset and held it up to his ear. "It's very, very cold here," a voice that he didn't recognize said slowly, "but if Laura's Lover will meet her at 947, he'll be delighted. The Indian's friends are wearing cavalry blue now, but since the house cats have long ears, they can't play." After a short pause, the message was repeated. "It's very, very cold here, but..."

Reese grinned. How in hell had Major Snow learned about Laura? "It's a message for me from the Iceman."

"What kind of message, sir?" the RTO asked. "It doesn't make sense."

"It's a World War II-style clear code meant specifically for me," Reese explained. "He's trying to tell me that Pierce is suited up and ready to come to our rescue if we need it. Switch over to 94.7. That's one of our bootleg channels."

As soon as Torres changed frequency, Reese keyed the mike. "Iceman, Iceman, this is Laura's Lover, over." He felt more than a little stupid using that particular call sign, but it had to be done.

"This is Iceman Control on 94.7," a new voice answered. "Stand by for the Iceman."

A second later Snow's distinctive voice came over the handset. "Laura's Lover, this is Iceman. What's your location? Over."

Reese quickly told the operations officer where they were and what Santelli had discovered on his brief recon of the airstrip.

"Roger," Snow answered. "Be advised that higher is very concerned because you have been out of contact with them. I informed them that you have equipment problems. I advise you to have continued equipment problems and stay on this frequency until you have recovered the package. Then contact me on Black Snake push for the extraction. Over.''

"This is Lover, wilco. Over.''

"Also,'' Snow continued, "the Indian is standing by with a one-hour echo tango alpha, but he will need a secure DZ. I am also trying to put together some Tac Air cover for your extraction. Over.''

Reese smiled. The Iceman had somehow managed to round up reinforcements and air support on the sly. That sounded more like the legendary Hungarian he had heard about. "Roger, I'll give you a call when I need them. Over.''

"Iceman, keep me informed. Out.''

Reese quickly called the team together to tell them about the call. "The Iceman's helping us CYA,'' Reese explained. "He's also got Pierce and some of the Nungs suited up and standing by in case we need help.''

Kowalski grinned. "About fuckin' time!''

"But what about the assholes at MACV?'' Hammer asked. "Can't they monitor his radio traffic and hear what he's doing?''

"Actually not,'' Reese explained. "He's using a bootleg channel. We have several of these that we reserve for SOG black ops, and he's also using a retransmission site to call me instead of going through Hillsboro. That way, as far as anyone at MACV knows, we're still running around lost in the jungle with a dead radio.''

"No wonder they call you guys 'Sneaky Petes,'" the Air Force officer said, smiling. "You don't even play fair with your own headquarters."

"We stick it up their asses, too, when we have to," Reese said, smiling back. "Sometimes that's the only thing we can do to protect ourselves when the air-conditioned warriors back in Saigon get in the way of operational realities."

"I'd better get going on the recon," Santelli said. "If we're going to bring Pierce in, we need to know what he'll be jumping into."

"Get going, Jack," Reese said. "But keep out of sight. If you get into trouble, we won't be able to bail you out."

Santelli grinned. "We'll be careful. You can count on that shit."

MAJOR YERMOLAV MOPPED the sweat from his face and reached for his canteen. Even with the heat, so far today they had made good time along the narrow mountain road. Getting a real night's sleep for a change seemed to have calmed his stomach down, as well; he'd had to stop along the trail only once so far. Maybe he would survive his trip to this miserable country without shitting himself to death, after all.

He vowed that once he got back to Rodina, Mother Russia, he was never going to leave her soil again. But he knew that if another opportunity came to salvage an American airplane, he would be tempted to go. The lure of being able to advance Soviet aviation technology at the expense of the Yankees was overpowering.

He prayed, though, that if he ever did have to go on another aircraft salvage mission, it would be to someplace that was halfway civilized and not this miserable part of the world again. He did have to admit, though, that the trip had been very worthwhile. The low-light television technology he'd taken from the Spectre alone was worth millions of rubles in research funds the Soviet air force wouldn't have to spend. The two prisoners could prove to be almost as valuable because they knew how to use the advanced equipment.

When he got them back to the Soviet Union, he would try to see that they were treated as well as the German engineers who had been taken to Russia at the end of World War II. The German scientists had been essential in building the advanced jets and rockets that had allowed Russia to stand up to the Western air forces in the early postwar era. Without their valuable work the Soviet air force would never have caught up with the rapidly advancing American aviation technology of the late forties and early fifties.

As it was now, the latest Soviet bomber and fighter aircraft were as advanced as their American opponents. It was only in the area of ground-attack weaponry that the Russians lagged behind. And that, of course, was why Yermolav had been sent on this mission.

Seeing Lieutenant Vinh hurrying toward him, he wondered what the hell it was this time. If he ever had the misfortune to have to do a job in Vietnam again, he sure as hell would insist he had final authority over who would command his security team. Vinh's professional paranoia was getting on his nerves.

"Comrade Major," the Vietnamese officer said, coming to attention, "I just received information that an infantry platoon of the Glorious People's Army is moving to meet us. They should catch up with us within the hour."

"Why are they doing that?" Yermolav asked. "We are almost at the airfield. If we keep on going, we'll be there before dark."

"My command has sent them to protect us, Comrade Major. They have learned there is a Yankee unit operating in this area and they think it's tracking us."

"How do they know that?"

"They talked to the Laotian boatman who took them across the Xe Ban Foi River. He told them he let the Yankees off on the western bank and said they continued on to the west. Also, they have lost contact with a unit of Laotian freedom fighters who were in the area along the border that they think the Yankees passed through."

Yermolav shrugged. There had been absolutely no sign of any Americans, but if the monkeys wanted to waste their time chasing phantoms, he couldn't care less. As long as they didn't slow him down and he could get a helicopter in quickly in the morning to take him and his prisoners to Hanoi, he didn't care how many Vietnamese troops escorted him.

"They can do what they like," he told Vinh. "Just as long as we reach the airfield before nightfall."

"Yes, Comrade Major."

SANTELLI AND WHISKEY didn't have to go all the way up into the hills to make contact with the Russian and his North Vietnamese escort. After being on the run for a little over two hours, they came upon the rear elements of an NVA infantry platoon in full combat gear moving up into the hills toward the Russian.

Ducking back into the bush, they watched the North Vietnamese as they started up the mountain road at a quick march. As soon as the enemy drag man had passed, Santelli and Whiskey broke cover and followed. Half a mile farther the platoon stopped in a grove of trees.

Watching from a safe distance, Santelli got an idea and turned to the Nung beside him. "Whiskey, how'd you like to sneak up there and see if you can hear what they're talking about?"

The Nung smiled. He liked sneaking around listening in on the Cong. Dropping his assault harness, but keeping his M-16, Whiskey dashed across the road and slipped into the bush along the NVA's side of the trail. There was nothing for Santelli to do while he was gone except wait and be prepared to cover him if something went wrong.

The time passed slowly, and he checked his watch every couple of minutes, but just as the NVA unit got ready to move out again, Whiskey slipped back and Santelli saw that he had a big grin on his face.

"*Trung Si,*" the Nung said, "the Cong say they not happy to climb the hills to meet the Russian. They say the long nose afraid of his own shadow. They also say it will take them over two hours to reach them and they won't get to the airfield until right before dark.''

Santelli smiled. That timetable meant there was still plenty of time to get their reinforcements in. Since he didn't have a radio, Santelli decided to go back to tell Reese what Whiskey had overheard. "Come on," he said, "we need to go back and tell the captain about this.''

While waiting for Santelli and the Nung to return, Reese had kept a close eye on the Tron Noi airfield. So far he had seen only two men when the radio watch had been changed. The rest were probably still taking their midday siesta. He expected that would change within the next hour or so. As the day got cooler, the enemy would start stirring as they prepared for their evening meal. If he was going to try to take the place, he needed to do it soon.

Wilson came up and crouched in the bush beside him. "Captain," he said, "the LT's coming back.''

Reese was surprised. Either the Russian had made better time than he had figured or something had gone wrong, badly wrong. He backed out of his observation point and returned to the team's defensive position.

It was plain to see that Santelli and Whiskey had been running to bring their information back. Both were soaked in sweat.

"What is it?" Reese asked as the lieutenant squatted beside him, panting to catch his breath.

"We've got us another problem, Captain," Santelli gasped. "The Russian's picked up an escort. We ran into an enemy platoon headed into the hills to join up with them."

"How many were there?"

"We counted twenty-six."

"Shit!" With the fifteen or twenty NVA the villagers had reported to be with the Russian, that meant he was facing at least forty enemy troops. There was just no way he could do anything against that kind of opposition with his seven-man team. It was time to get Pierce and his reinforcements involved. As the team sergeant had predicted, he needed the old Indian.

He turned to Torres. "Hand me the radio."

17

Tron Noi Airfield

While Santelli and Whiskey drank deeply from their canteens and splashed water on their faces to cool off, Reese tried to get back into communication with Major Snow. "Iceman, Iceman," he radioed, "this is Laura's Lover, over."

"This is Iceman Control," the retrans operator answered. "Wait one for the Iceman."

A moment later the operations officer was on the air. "This is the Iceman. Go ahead."

"This is Laura's Lover. It's time we got the Indians involved. The package has picked up an additional escort. We're facing at least forty hostiles and are going to need help before they arrive late this afternoon. I suggest a low-altitude drop on the bird's nest. Also bring enough Sky Hooks for the package and the three birdmen. Be advised that one of them is wounded. Over."

"Is the bird's nest secure? Over."

"It will be by the time they get here."

"Roger, they're on their way now. I will get back to you later with an exact echo tango alpha. Iceman out."

Hammer had overheard Reese's end of the conversation, but hadn't been able to decipher all of the slang and clear code the team leader had used. "Now what in hell are you planning to do?" he asked.

"It's simple," Reese answered. "In about an hour or so, my team sergeant is going to make a parachute drop on the airfield, bringing Mike Force reinforcements with him. And he's also bringing enough Sky Hook gear to get you and your people out after we get them back."

"Sky Hook?" Hammer asked. "What in hell's that?"

Reese grinned. "Believe me, Nails, you're going to love it. Have you ever ridden in a balloon?"

Hammer slowly shook his head. "You bastards are going to get me killed yet."

"The Sky Hook won't kill you, but what we have to do in the next thirty minutes might earn you a bullet badge for sure."

"What's that?"

Reese pointed to the airfield. "We have to go down there and wipe out those NVA so Pierce can use the runway for a drop zone."

"Oh, shit!"

Reese quickly got the team together to work out an attack plan. Even though the NVA garrison seemed to be rear-area troops and not battle-wise veteran infantry, there were still too damned many of them and they were armed. To overcome the difference in numbers Reese's attack would have to be swift and overpowering. And with Pierce due to arrive soon, it had to be done quickly.

The plan he came up with was simple. First, they would take out as many of them as they could without shooting. Once discovered, they would unleash everything to overwhelm the rest as quickly as possible. They also had to be careful not to start any fires. A plume of smoke would tip off the Russian that something was wrong. The briefing was quick and the team had no questions. They had all made this kind of raid many times before and they knew the drill.

As they got back into their rucks and checked their weapons, Reese turned to Hammer. "Listen, Nails," he said, "I want you to stick close to me when we get down there—real close. Do exactly what I do when I do it, but don't shoot until we're discovered."

Hammer nodded, his jaw set. Even though he had survived the ambush against the Pathet Lao and was now a "combat veteran" of sorts, he knew he wasn't really ready for something like this. He acutely felt his lack of training and, even more important, his lack of battle-tuned combat reflexes. He had seen how these men fought and knew that most of what they did under fire was sheer instinct and reflex. Since he didn't have those trained instincts and reflexes, all he could do was follow Reese's orders, keep a close eye on him and try real hard to keep from doing something stupid.

Within minutes Santelli and Kowalski slipped down the knoll, followed closely by Hotchkiss and Whiskey. Reese, Hammer, Torres and Wilson brought up the rear. They swung to the south, keeping well out of sight as they worked around to the far end of the airfield. In fifteen minutes they had reached their assault positions in the bush right beyond the mess hall.

Except for a single man stoking the fires under the pots of water, bringing them to a boil for the evening's rice, the place looked deserted. Reese caught Whiskey's eye and made a slashing motion with a finger across his neck. The Nung nodded.

Leaving Hotchkiss behind to cover him, Whiskey crept up on the mess hall. Carefully placing his M-16 on the ground, the Nung drew his razor-sharp Ka-Bar knife and silently slipped up behind the cook.

The cook was so busy preparing the meal that he had no idea he was being stalked until Whiskey's arm snapped around his head and clamped tightly over his mouth. The knife slammed into the NVA's kidneys, and the Nung gave it a savage twist. Held upright by Whiskey's arm, the cook's feet kicked in the dust, but he quickly went limp.

Lowering him, the Nung rolled the body out of sight under a table. Recovering his rifle, he took up a firing position beside the cinder-block fire pit and waved Hotchkiss forward. The sergeant dashed up and dropped beside him, his M-16 at the ready.

Under the cover of Hotchkiss's and Whiskey's rifles Santelli and Kowalski stepped out of the bush and raced for the garrison's sleeping quarters. Ducking beside the open barracks door, both men took off fragmentation grenades from their ammo pouches. Holding the safety spoons down, they pulled the pins and took up their rifles again.

Leaving Wilson in the bush to provide long-range cover, Reese, Hammer and Torres rushed for the radio shack and dropped into cover behind its back wall. Now that everyone was in place it was show time. Looking over at Santelli, Reese shot him a thumbs-up.

Catching Reese's signal, Santelli nodded at Ski, and the two men released their grenade spoons, initiating the fuze trains on the frags. Silently counting off three seconds, they pitched the grenades into the barracks and flattened on their bellies. The pair of M-26 frags exploded two seconds later, sending their deadly shards of metal flying into the bodies of the sleeping men.

Jumping up, the two men stuck the barrels of their weapons through the open door and sent a blaze of 5.56 mm fire into the survivors. When their bolts locked back on empty magazines, they pitched two more grenades in and ducked back to change magazines.

When Santelli and Kowalski's grenades exploded, the North Vietnamese radioman grabbed his SKS rifle and ran out of his shack to see what was going on. Racing around the corner, he ran straight into a short burst of fire from Reese's CAR-15. The 5.56 mm rounds stitched him up the front, and he went down, flat on his face.

When Santelli and Kowalski came up again, three survivors of the grenade attack opened up on them with their SKSs. The men ducked back down as bullets smashed into the doorframe. Snatching his last grenade, Ski ripped off a burst around the corner and pitched the grenade in.

When the enemy saw the grenade, they dashed out the back door of the barracks, shooting blindly as they ran. Firing from the mess hall, Hotchkiss and Whiskey quickly cut them down and, as suddenly as it had begun, the battle was over.

The team's surprise had been complete. In less than three minutes all the North Vietnamese garrison had been killed and none of the American team had been hit.

With Ski covering him, Santelli walked through the barracks building. A thin wisp of smoke rose from the muzzle of the CAR-15 in his right hand and his finger was still poised on the trigger. Midway through the row of bunks one of the NVA victims of the grenades moaned. Santelli quickly put a bullet in his head and continued on.

"All clear," he reported when he stepped out of the other end of the building.

Outside, Hammer approached the bodies of the three NVA who had run out of the barracks building. Rolling the first body over, he saw that his NVA was still alive. The man had taken several rounds in the belly and held his hands pressed over the wounds. His eyes opened and, when he saw Hammer, he held his bloodied hands up in a gesture for mercy.

"Over here!" Hammer called out, holding his AK steady on him. "I've found one of them still alive!"

Whiskey hurried over, his M-16 held at the ready. He stopped short of the NVA and looked at Hammer.

"He's still alive," the Air Force officer repeated.

With one smooth movement the Nung drew the Ka-Bar knife from the sheath on his assault harness and stepped up to the NVA. Stabbing the wounded man's throat, he gave the blade a twist. The NVA's eyes opened wide and a scream gurgled in his throat.

With a toothy grin the Nung wiped the blade clean on the NVA's shirt and resheathed it. "No sweat, *Thieu Ta* Nails. This Cong, he dead now, too."

Hammer turned his head away and fought down the urge to vomit. This was the second time he had watched a man die from cold steel in the past two days, but he still wasn't used to it. Also, he hadn't yet made the adjustment to the "take no prisoners" attitude of the SF team. He realized, however, that killing the wounded NVA had actually been a humane act. There was no way the man would have been able to survive until his own people could get to him.

The Nung dragged the body to the barracks and dumped it inside with the others.

While the team searched the bodies Reese quickly set up his new command post in the NVA's radio shacks. Pierce was in the air already, winging his way north, and he needed to know that his DZ had been secured.

"Iceman, Iceman," he radioed the retrans station, "this is Laura's Lover, over."

"This is the Iceman. Go ahead."

"This is Laura's Lover. Be advised the bird's nest is secure. I say again, the bird's nest is secure. Over."

"Roger, the Indian is on his way. Expect him in forty-five minutes, over."

"Roger, we'll be waiting. Out."

Leaving Torres with the radio, Reese walked over to the mess hall where the rest of the team had gathered after policing up the battlefield. Santelli was munching on another banana while Whiskey put rice in the boiling water to cook. Even though they didn't have much time to eat, Reese had to admit that a hot meal wasn't a bad idea; he couldn't remember when he had last had a freshly cooked hot meal. Lurps and C-rations were nutritious but they were boring as hell.

Sitting at one of the tables, Hammer watched the team go about fixing an early dinner. He never ceased to be amazed by the attitude of the Special Forces team. They had just wiped out an enemy force twice their size and, while waiting to take on an even bigger NVA unit, were taking time out to cook as if they were on a Boy Scout outing.

The Air Force officer had to admit, though, that the smell of the cooking food made his mouth water. Unlike the Special Forces men, he wasn't used to eating field rations and didn't see how in hell the team could exist on them day in and day out. But, as he had learned in the past three days, a man could get used to anything.

"Want a cup of coffee, sir?" Hotchkiss asked as he walked up to Hammer with a steaming canteen cup.

Hammer took the cup. "Thanks."

"Cream or sugar, sir?"

"No thanks. I take mine bareback."

Hotchkiss laughed. "We'll make a grunt out of you yet, Major."

The hot coffee tasted good, real good. The Air Force officer had almost forgotten just how good coffee could taste. After spending three days with Reese and his men, he realized more than ever the vast difference between his war and theirs. To him a hot cup of freshly brewed coffee was something he could have anytime he wanted. His crew had even had a coffeepot hooked up in their Spectre. To these guys, however, coffee was usually a vile brew of vitamin-fortified, powdered C-rations coffee heated luke-warm in a canteen cup over a ball of burning C-4 plastic explosive. Maybe that was what made them so tough. You had to be a real man to drink that shit.

"How long have you been in the Special Forces, Sergeant?" Hammer asked.

Hotchkiss thought for a moment. "About five years, I guess, sir," he grinned. "Time flies when you're having fun."

Hammer noticed that the sergeant winced when he reached for something in his rucksack. "How's that wound?"

"The wound's okay. But that rib hurts like a moth-erfucker. I think I hit it again during the assault."

Hammer remembered seeing Hotchkiss slam into the ground when he dived for cover. "You'd better have Wilson take another look at that."

Hotchkiss shook his head. "There's not much he can do for me here. I just need to take a couple of weeks off and take it easy while it heals." He grinned broadly. "A couple of weeks in Nha Trang, like the captain promised me."

Whiskey announced that the rice was ready, and Hammer stood in line with the others for his share. The steaming food smelled good as he sat down across from Kowalski and started to dig in.

"You want a little *nuoc-mam* on that?" Kowalski asked, holding out a bottle of the amber-colored, oily fluid. "It's pretty good on rice."

"Oh, no, you don't," Hammer said in mock horror. "I may be an FNG as far as you're concerned, but even I've heard all about that stuff. Rotten fish never did turn me on."

Kowalski grinned. "You don't ever want to run into my ex-wife then."

Hammer chuckled at the old joke. The situation couldn't be that serious if Ski was laid back enough to tell a bad joke like that. From what he had seen of the Special Forces men so far, it took quite a bit to break their cool.

The team was just finishing eating when Torres stuck his head out of the radio shack. "Captain!" he called. "They're inbound."

18

Tron Noi Airfield

Reese hurried into the open and saw a dark speck in the sky rapidly approaching from the south. As it came closer, he could make out the distinctive shape of the high-winged, four-engined C-130 Hercules transport plane. He turned to Torres and reached for the handset. "What's their call sign?"

"Indian Five Seven."

"Indian Five Seven," Reese radioed, "this is Laura's Lover. We have you in sight. Your DZ runs west to east. Ground wind is from the west, but negligible. Make your approach from the south and exit the DZ to the south. Do not overfly the area to the north of the DZ and stay down low until you're well clear of the area. How copy? Over."

"Five Seven, roger. Understand southern approach and exit. Make drop from west to east. Do not overfly the north and hug the trees going out. I have your DZ in sight now. Pop smoke and stand by."

"Pop a smoke," Reese ordered.

Kowalski grabbed a smoke grenade from his rucksack, pulled the pin and tossed it out onto the runway. The grenade ignited with a pop, and a thick column of green smoke billowed into the still air.

"This is Lover, smoke out."

"Five Seven. I have your lime, over."

"Roger, green smoke. You're clear to drop."

"This is Five Seven on final," the pilot radioed as he banked the Herky for his final approach. "Stand by for the drop."

Leveling out, the camouflaged Herky dropped until she was only six hundred feet off the ground as she approached the airstrip. Both her flaps and her rear ramp door were down for the drop as the pilot throttled back to 130 knots airspeed. Making a parachute drop at that low altitude was tricky enough, but trying to exit the aircraft at a faster airspeed could get someone hurt.

The troop transport hadn't yet reached the runway before the first man-size shape fell from the open ramp door. Almost instantly a parachute canopy blossomed open about five hundred feet above the ground. The first jumper was quickly followed by over a dozen more. The men hanging below the parachutes barely had time to assume a good landing position before their jungle boots hit the ground.

After the paratroopers jumped, four orange cargo parachutes opened, gently lowering several crates to the ground. In seconds the Nung reinforcements and their equipment were all on the ground.

Keeping low, the Herky pilot sucked up his flaps, closed his ramp door and advanced his throttles to full military power. "This is Five Seven," he radioed. "I'm clear and outbound."

"This is Lover. Thanks, Five Seven."

"De nada."

Reese and his team hurried onto the runway to help gather the parachutes. "Welcome to North Vietnam," he greeted his team sergeant.

"I'm getting too old for this shit, Captain," Pierce said as he unbuckled his parachute harness and started pulling the collapsed canopy toward him.

"Just think, Sarge, you'll get to put a combat drop star on your jump badge now."

"I already got one of them from Korea. And you know they're never going to let this one count, anyway."

Reese knew that was all too true. While combat parachute jumps were a big deal in the Regular Army, SOG teams made combat jumps all the time. But like everything else about SOG's secret war, they never received recognition for them. While the Mike Force had been awarded the coveted combat drop stars for their jumps in South Vietnam, none of the SOG team drops counted.

While some of the Nungs fanned out to secure the drop zone, others quickly broke open the drop canisters and retrieved their heavy weapons—M-60s and Russian RPG rocket launchers. Even though the U.S. Army had an antitank rocket launcher in its inventory, the M-72 LAW, the weapon was rarely carried on SOG cross-border operations.

Although manufactured in the United States, the LAW was a real piece of shit. Not only did it misfire most of the time, its warhead was only half the size of the Russian weapon. Its range was also less than half of the RPG. When Special Forces teams needed a dependable rocket launcher to take out bunkers or machine gun nests, they used captured RPGs.

Along with the weapons and Sky Hook equipment, an ammunition resupply for Reese's team had been included in the drop. The team quickly loaded their empty magazines, slung extra bandoliers of ammo around their necks and replenished their hand grenades.

While this was going on Reese and Pierce huddled over the map as Reese tried to bring his team sergeant up to date on the situation.

"So," Pierce said, shaking his head when Reese was finished, "you're telling me we don't really know how many of them we're up against and we don't have any idea when they're going to show up."

"That's about it, Sarge," Reese admitted. "It's been that sort of operation right from the start. Ever since we found out the plane had been stripped, we've been trying to play catch-up. And since MACV cut us off, we've been running blind to boot."

"Someday, sir," Pierce growled, "we've got to get us a straightforward mission. Something we can prepare for and execute like we know what we're doing."

Reese laughed. "This is the wrong war and we're in the wrong organization for that kind of thing. Remember, Sarge, this is Nam and you're wearing a green beret."

"Don't I know it, sir."

Reese folded his map and stuffed it back into his pants pocket. "We'd better get going," he said, glancing at his watch. "I want to get to those hills before they do. Otherwise we're going to have to fight a running gun battle with those little bastards and somebody's going to get hurt."

"I'll get 'em moving."

MAJOR YERMOLAV WAS feeling better than he had since this abortive operation had started. They were on the downhill leg of the mountain road and would soon reach the plain. Once they were on the flat ground it would take only an hour or so to get to the Tron Noi airstrip, which meant they would arrive well before dark. He was so close to getting out of this miserable place that he could almost feel the long, hot shower he would take the second he got back to his hotel room in Hanoi.

Vinh's North Vietnamese infantry escort hadn't slowed them up at all. In fact, they had helped keep the pace he was setting. By alternating the men carrying the equipment and the wounded American's litter, they were making better time than before.

The Russian decided to drop back and tell his two American prisoners that their ordeal was almost at an end. Even though they were the enemies of his allies, they were still aviators, and the brotherhood of flyers was strong. As he had done from the beginning of the march, Yermolav saw that Sergeant Kegan was walking alongside the litter bearing his wounded comrade. The end of the noose around his neck was even tied to the litter.

Yermolav nodded toward Jones. "How is your comrade?"

Kegan shook his head. "He's not good, sir. I ran out of things to give him, and he needs to get to a doctor fast or he's going to lose that leg."

"We should be back in Hanoi tomorrow morning," the Russian said. "Then I will personally see that he receives proper medical attention."

"I hope he lasts that long, sir."

"So do I, Sergeant."

As Yermolav was turning to the front, his trained eyes caught the speck of a large aircraft in the distance. He squinted as he tried to identify the model, but it was too far away. Estimating the distance, however, told him that it was a large plane, larger than anything the North Vietnamese would have in the area. With the Yankee fighters owning the sky over North Vietnam, the NVAF was very careful where it flew its small fleet of transports and bombers.

It occurred to Yermolav that the plane might be some type of Yankee reconnaissance aircraft looking for him and the salvaged fire control equipment. From the way the Americans had responded so far he wouldn't put it past them to do something like that. But even if they were spotted, there was little the Yankees could do except send in fighter planes to destroy the gear. Under the circumstances that certainly was what the Soviet air force would do.

He quickly put that idea from his mind, however, and decided not to mention it to Vinh. If the paranoid North Vietnamese lieutenant thought the Yankees were hunting him from the sky, he would just use it as an excuse to move off the road and try to stay out of sight. That would only slow them, and the Russian wouldn't put up with that. Even if he couldn't get a helicopter down from Hanoi this evening, he was looking forward to sleeping on a real bed again.

IT WAS GETTING into late afternoon when Reese's newly reinforced unit moved out. If they hurried, they would meet the NVA when they came out of the hills and started down into the plain. As yet, he didn't have a firm battle plan; that would have to wait until he saw the ground he would have to fight on. But he knew he had to beat the North Vietnamese to the open terrain at the bottom of the hill.

As they covered ground at double time, Reese radioed Major Snow. Now that Pierce was on the ground and they were moving toward the conclusion of the operation, it was time to put the final pieces on the board.

"Iceman, Iceman," he radioed, "this is Laura's Lover, over."

"Iceman Control, wait one, out."

"This is Iceman," came Snow's distinctive voice over the handset. "Go ahead."

"This is Lover," Reese answered. "We're moving to contact now. Estimate a little over an hour until we reach them. Alert the Sky Hook people and the extraction bird. When we get the package back, we may have to get out of here in a big hurry. Over."

"Iceman, roger. I will get everything ready. I am still working on the Tac Air now and will get back to you when it's available. Out."

Half an hour later Reese's point elements reached the foothills and reported back that they had beaten the North Vietnamese to the area. As soon as the column closed up, the Nungs formed a defensive perimeter in the scattered bush and trees while Reese surveyed the terrain at the base of the hills through his field glasses.

Immediately he saw that it was a better battleground than it had looked on the map. The twisting mountain road straightened out at the bottom of the hill and ran through an area of large boulders, scattered trees and scrub. Since he had extra radios now, he could split up his unit and still communicate with them. That would allow him to put together a rather complicated plan that should let them recover the fire control equipment from the Spectre and the prisoners while he engaged the NVA troops.

Laying out his map on the ground, Reese called his NCOs to him for a quick briefing. "Okay," he said, "here's the plan. Jack, I want you to take Kowalski and eight Nungs and do an end run behind them. Your job is to grab the fire control equipment and the prisoners while we chew 'em up. Once you've got them, get back to the airstrip fast, rig the Sky Hooks and prepare to get them out of here as soon as the planes show up. While you're doing that we'll hold them off here and try to get some Tac Air in to give us a hand."

Santelli nodded. That was his kind of assignment—something with dash and danger but with the chance of a great reward if he pulled it off.

"Sergeant Pierce," Reese continued, "I want you to take Wilson, Hotchkiss and half of the Nungs across the road and hold down the right flank. Put them out so that you'll have the first two hundred meters of the road as a killing zone."

Pierce nodded.

"I'll take Torres and Nails and the rest of the strikers with me," Reese continued. "We'll hold down the left side. I want to let the Dinks get well down onto the flat and then we'll tear them a new asshole. Get your RPG gunners sighted in on the rear of the killing zone and have your gunner ready to take them in front. Make sure everybody holds their fire until I give the signal. I don't want those little bastards taking cover on that hillside where they can shoot down on us."

Reese looked hard at each of his sergeants in turn. "This shouldn't be all that difficult. We've got surprise on our side and we aren't outnumbered that badly. But if we find out that we've bitten off more than we can chew, we're not going to pull any kind of Alamo number here. We'll fall back on the airstrip and scream for help. Does anyone have any questions?"

"What do you want us to do about the Russian?" Santelli asked.

"I'd like you to take him alive, if you can," Reese said. "But if he presents any kind of problem, he's fair game—waste him."

Santelli grinned.

"Okay, people," Reese said, "if there's nothing else, let's do it."

Santelli quickly picked the men for his rescue mission and moved out into the hills. As soon as Santelli moved out, Reese and Pierce quickly moved their men into position. With the twenty men Pierce had brought with him, the odds against them weren't as bad as they had been before, but they still needed to have the element of surprise.

19

Tron Noi Airfield

As the North Vietnamese point element moved down into the plain, Major Yermolav didn't forget the aircraft he had seen earlier. While he thought of himself as being every bit as brave as the next man, he also had an appreciation of the need for caution on a battlefield. There was always the off chance that he had been spotted by the plane and the Yankees would have fighter bombers waiting for them to move into the open where they could be easily attacked. He let Vinh move down with the main body of the infantry while he stayed well to the rear of the column with the salvaged electronic gear and his two Yankee prisoners.

He could see the Tron Noi airstrip in the distance; it looked deserted. He assumed the garrison was more than likely still taking their afternoon naps. No wonder these monkeys couldn't build a civilized nation—they were too busy sleeping.

HIDING BEHIND a large boulder, Reese watched through his field glasses as the NVA point element came down the trail onto open ground. As he had hoped, since the enemy was on home turf and was so close to the airstrip, they thought they were safe and weren't paying close attention to their surroundings. They were bunched up nicely, too, and that would make his job that much easier.

He scanned the advancing troops, looking for the American captives and the Russian. All he could see were the NVA hard-hat infantry, but that was good. That probably meant the prisoners were at the rear of the column where Santelli could get to them easily once the firefight began.

He glanced across the trail and saw that Pierce's men were all under cover and the sergeant was looking at him, waiting for the signal. Everything was in place and he had only to wait a few more minutes until the main body of the NVA moved onto the ambush killing zone. But, no matter how many times he had done this, those few minutes were always the longest minutes of his life. Even though he was confident he would pull this off, he knew someday he'd fuck up and die in one of these ambushes. Brushing those thoughts aside, he waited patiently until the front of the enemy column was well within the killing zone.

At his signal the four Nung RPG gunners fired as one. The launch charges propelled the 85 mm rocket grenades out of the launchers. A few meters out of the muzzles the secondary flight charges ignited, speeding the RPG grounds to their targets.

The shaped charge rockets, designed to kill tanks, also made good antipersonnel weapons. Shrapnel from the exploding warheads tore into the front of the enemy column while Reese's M-60 machine guns opened up and took out the rest of the lead element.

The NVA had been caught flat-footed, but they quickly recovered and deployed in the bush. A storm of return fire, including a pair of RPD machine guns and a couple of RPGs of their own, immediately broke out.

Though Reese's men had the advantage of position, the NVA still had the numbers. Whoever was in command was on his toes and immediately started maneuvering his men around to Pierce's flank. Those still coming down the hill hurried to join the combat. Furious firefights broke out as the NVA probed to find a way out of the trap.

While the NVA were drawn down into the firefight on the plain, Santelli quickly led his small team up the hill. Breaking out onto the trail, he glanced uphill and saw the four NVA carrying the fire control equipment on poles over their shoulders, and their two relief men hurrying downhill to join their comrades.

Ducking back into the rocks, Santelli alerted his Nungs and quickly set up a hasty ambush. When the six NVA entered the killing zone three minutes later, a storm of fire cut them down before any of them had a chance to get off even a single shot.

Dashing onto the trail, the Nungs picked up the poles carrying the equipment and carried it back into cover while Santelli got on the radio to Reese. "We have the equipment," he reported. "But the prisoners aren't here. Apparently they're still with the Russian and he's somewhere down there with the Dinks."

"Find 'em!" Reese ordered. "Leave the fucking equipment and find 'em."

Regardless of what Reese had said, Santelli didn't want to have to climb the hill again, so he had the Nungs take the equipment with them. Not wanting to move down the open road, he dropped back behind the cover of the rocks as he made his way down.

Down on the plain Reese's men were holding their own against the NVA, but just barely. The initial ambush had evened the odds somewhat, but there were still too damn many of them, and they weren't backing off. Pierce was having a particularly difficult time on his flank, and Reese sent four of his men over to assist him. Even with the covering fire one of the four was hit as he tried to cross the road.

Reese was slamming a fresh magazine into his CAR-15 when Torres held out the radio handset. "It's the major!" he yelled over the rattle of small-arms fire.

Reese took the handset. "This is Laura's Lover. Go."

"This is the Iceman," Snow answered. "Be advised a flight of four Spads are inbound to your location at this time. Go public now and contact Gypsy Lead through Hillsboro on your old push. Over."

"Roger, out."

Quickly switching frequencies, he keyed the handset. "Hillsboro, Hillsboro," he radioed. "This is Gray Ghost One One, Gray Ghost One One, over."

"This is Hillsboro. Go."

"This is One One. Patch me through to Gypsy Lead ASAP."

An instant later the Spad flight leader was on the radio. "This is Gypsy Lead. Go."

"This is Ghost One One. We're in contact to the north of the Tron Noi airfield and need assistance ASAP."

"Lead roger, that's what we're here for. What's your situation?"

Reese quickly gave the pilot his position and the positions of the NVA. "I can't pop smoke for you. It'll give my location away to the dinks."

"Lead roger, understand. We're rolling in now."

Their engines screaming, the first pair of Air Force Super Spads dived on the attacking NVA. CBUs, Cluster Bomb Units, dropped off their underwing pylons and burst open in the air. Dozens of baseball-size bomblets fell free and rained down on the NVA. Each bomblet carried the explosive charge of a hand grenade and flung killing fragments to a radius of five meters when it detonated. Carpeting the base of the hill, the CBUs erupted in dozens of small explosions, but most of them didn't hit the NVA.

Seeing that the Spads were off their target because they didn't have FAC to direct them, Hammer put down his AK and started to ask Reese for the radio handset to direct the strike. Then he remembered the SR-10 survival radio in his pocket, brought it out and keyed the mike. "Gypsy Lead, this is Spectre Alpha on Guard channel. I'm with the unit in contact and will direct your strike. Over."

"Spectre Alpha, this is Lead. Where do you want it?"

With Hammer giving directions in a language the Spad pilots could easily understand, the second pair of Spads delivered their napalm canisters right on target and broke the attack. NVA with their uniforms on fire ran out of the bush directly into Reese's guns and were mercifully cut down.

Under Hammer's guidance the Spads sprayed HE shells from their 20 mm wing cannons as well as 2.75-inch rockets from the underwing pods. Under the concentrated air attack the surviving NVA turned on their heels and tried to flee east along the side of the hill. Reese's Nungs fired everything they had into the backs of the running NVA, adding to their panic. Only a few escaped.

MAJOR YERMOLAV CROUCHED behind a rock as the Skyraiders screamed down on Vinh's infantry at the base of the hill. With the smoke and dust thrown up by the bombs and rockets, he couldn't see exactly what was happening down there, but he knew it wasn't good. He had also heard the firing from the rear of the column and knew that a second American unit had ambushed the Vietnamese carrying the Spectre fire control equipment.

While Yermolav was trying to see what was happening at his rear, a wild-eyed Vinh ran back up the road from the carnage below. The Vietnamese officer stopped, snatched up a fallen AK and ran to where the American prisoners were huddled behind a rock. Pulling back on the charging handle to chamber a round, he triggered off a burst from the hip.

"Major!" Kegan screamed as he threw his body over Jones to protect him. "Look out!"

Yermolav spun around, the Makarov pistol in his hands. Taking up a two-handed firing stance, he quickly triggered three shots. The first two 9 mm rounds took Vinh in the chest, stopping him cold in his tracks. The third shot hit him right between the eyes. The AK fell from his nerveless fingers and he crumpled to the ground.

"Are you hurt?" Yermolav asked the American.

Kegan shook his head. "No."

Yermolav glanced down to the plain where the Yankee fighter bombers and infantry were chewing up the last of Vinh's North Vietnamese. The Russian was a Communist, but he was a realist. He knew that in a few short minutes the Yankees would start looking for him and his two captives. He also knew that a trigger-happy Yankee would love an excuse to add a Russian officer to his body count. The mission was a failure, but there was still a chance he could get out of this alive.

Reaching down, Yermolav picked up the dead Vietnamese officer's assault rifle and handed it to the Air Force sergeant. "Here," he said, "take this. Use it if anyone else tries to kill you. I am going down there to talk to your comrades."

With a puzzled look Kegan took the rifle. He started to bring it up to fire on the Russian, but stopped halfway and dropped the muzzle. "Thanks," he said.

"You will be safe if you stay here," Yermolav said. "I will bring your comrades up to you."

The Russian started down the hill, keeping well under cover. After surviving this long, he didn't want to be killed now. Spotting a flash of movement twenty meters in front of him, he dropped behind a rock. "American commander!" he called out as loudly as he could. "I am a Soviet air force officer! I want to talk to you!"

Santelli ducked when he heard the Russian shout. "What do you want?"

"I want to talk."

Santelli hesitated. "I'm coming up!" He waved Kowalski up to him. "Cover me."

"You're not going up there, are you, LT?"

"Sure," Santelli said, "why not? The man says he wants to talk."

"I don't trust the bastard," Kowalski said as he slapped a fresh magazine into his M-16 and adjusted his rear sight. "I'm going to keep a bead on that fucker when he steps out, and if he even twitches, I'm going to waste his ass."

Santelli clapped him on the shoulder. "You do that, Sarge."

Holding his CAR-15 muzzle down, Santelli stepped out into the open and started up into the rocks. At the same time a stocky blond man in an olive-brown uniform stepped out and stood still, waiting for him. Santelli stopped a few feet in front of him, his CAR pointed down, his finger still on the trigger.

"Are you the American commander?" the Russian asked in heavily accented English.

Santelli shook his head. "I'm the second-in-command, First Lieutenant Jack Santelli, United

States Special Forces, but I speak for my commander.''

The Russian saluted. "Major Yuri Yermolav of the Soviet air force."

Santelli didn't return his salute, but kept his right hand on the pistol grip of his CAR-15 and his finger on the trigger. "What can I do for you, Major?"

"I wish to surrender."

Santelli snapped the muzzle of his weapon up to cover him. "Okay," he said, "if you want to surrender, take your left hand and slowly open your pistol holster."

Yermolav did as he was told.

"Now," Santelli said when he saw the blue steel butt of the Makarov, "take the pistol out slowly and drop it on the ground."

Using only his thumb and first finger, the Russian pulled the weapon clear of his holster and let it fall.

Holding the CAR on him, Santelli picked up the pistol, stuffed it into his pant pocket, then quickly patted the Russian down for hidden weapons. "Okay," he asked, stepping back, "where are those two Americans you captured?"

Yermolav pointed to the jumble of boulders farther up the hillside behind him. "They are back there."

Without taking his eyes off the Russian Santelli waved Kowalski and the Nungs up to him. "They'd better still be alive."

"They are," Yermolav promised.

"Show me."

Putting Yermolav in the care of two grinning Nungs with M-16s, Santelli signaled them to follow him up the hill. The Russian had surrendered and seemed to want to cooperate, but Santelli wasn't about to trust him until he saw the flyers.

A hundred meters up the hill the Russian stopped in front of the boulders. "Sergeant!" he called out softly. "I have brought your comrades."

Kegan eased out from cover, his AK at the ready.

"I'm Lieutenant Santelli. You guys okay?"

Kegan lowered the muzzle of his AK. "Jesus, am I glad to see you, sir."

"Are you okay?"

"I'm fine, sir," Kegan said wearily. "But Jonesy's in bad shape. He was hit in the leg and it's infected bad."

"We've got a medic with us," Santelli said. "And we'll be getting you guys outta here ASAP."

With two Nungs carrying each end of the litter, they quickly started back down the hill.

"Okay, Ivan," Santelli said, motioning with the muzzle of his CAR-15, "let's go meet my commander."

20

Tron Noi Airfield

Reese was directing a search of the battlefield when he saw Santelli's men hurrying through the bush with the litter bearing the wounded airman and the fire control gear. Walking in front of Santelli was a stocky blond man wearing a dark olive-brown uniform with blue epaulets and color tabs—the mysterious Russian they had been following for the past three days.

"Captain Reese," Santelli announced, "this is Major Yermolav of the Russian air force. He wisely decided to surrender and return our men to us."

Yermolav snapped to attention and saluted. Reese hesitated for a moment before returning the Russian's salute. Normally it wasn't healthy to salute in the field because it attracted attention from enemy snipers, but this was different. "I'm Captain Mike Reese, United States Special Forces."

"Major Yuri Yermolav. I am pleased to meet you, Captain."

Reese studied him for a moment. "You're a long way from home, aren't you, Major?"

Before the Russian could answer Hammer walked up to him. "Look at his feet, Reese," he growled as he snapped his AK up to zero in on Yermolav. "This fucker's wearing GI jungle boots."

Reese looked down and saw that the Russian was wearing U.S.-issue boots, obviously the boots that had been taken from the body near the Spectre wreck. Being an infantryman, Reese didn't have a problem with scrounging from the battlefield, but Hammer certainly seemed to. He still didn't fully appreciate the harsh realities of life in the field.

"He took those from Keats's body," Hammer said. "I ought to shoot him right here and now."

"Don't do it, sir!" Kegan shouted as he ran forward. "He saved our lives!"

"What do you mean?"

Kegan quickly explained how the Russian had kept Vinh from disposing of them on the trail, how he had ordered them to be fed and how he had killed the Vietnamese officer to protect them. "We owe our lives to him, sir. We really do."

Hammer released the Russian and stepped back. "Why did you do that?" he asked suspiciously.

Yermolav shrugged. "No civilized man mistreats prisoners of war."

"You're just following the Geneva Convention, right?" Hammer said sarcastically. "Shoot us down and then treat us well?"

"Okay, Nails," Reese said, stepping between the two men, "it's all over now. We've got your men now and we've got to get back to the airstrip."

Yermolav noted the wings on Hammer's uniform. "You were on the Spectre gunship, yes?"

Hammer's eyes narrowed. "Yes, I was."

"I am sorry."

"Fuck you." Hammer turned and walked away.

Back at the airfield, while Wilson and the Nung medic cared for their few casualties, Pierce and a team of Nungs laid out the Sky Hook gear and got ready to start evacuating the aircrew and equipment. As soon as the Air Force men showed up, they started helping them into the Sky Hook suits and harnesses.

The Fulton Surface-to-Air Recovery System gear was simple and straightforward. A man put on a flight suit that had a webbing harness built into it. The harness was clipped onto a long nylon rope that in turn was fastened to a small blimp-shaped helium balloon. The balloon was inflated from a helium canister included in the Sky Hook package. Once inflated, the balloon rose into the air, trailing the nylon rope. The retrieval aircraft flew into the rope under the balloon, a winch secured the rope and the man was quickly hauled up into the plane.

As soon as the men and the fire control equipment had been rigged, Reese got on the radio to Hillsboro to report that he was ready for the pickup. A moment later the pilot of the Sky Hook plane was on the horn. "Gray Ghost, this is Sky Hook on your fox mike. Over."

Reese took the handset. "This is Ghost One One. Go."

"This is Sky Hook. We're ready to start the pickup. Pop smoke, please."

Torres quickly pulled the pin and tossed out a smoke grenade. A column of green smoke rose almost vertically in the still air.

"This is Sky Hook. I have green smoke."

"This is One One. Roger, green," Reese answered. "We have five loads ready for you—two equipment and three personnel. One of the personnel is wounded and may not be able to assist in his pickup. Over."

"I copy five loads. Send the equipment loads first, so I can make sure everything's working up here. Over."

"One One, roger. The first load is coming up now."

Reese gave the signal and the first of the balloons was released. It quickly rose in the air and, due to its bullet shape and tail fins, it turned, nose into the wind. As soon as the rope was taut, Reese radioed to the pilot. "We're go on the first one."

"Roger," the pilot answered as he maneuvered his ship to come in from the front of the balloon. The modified C-130 retrieval ship was low enough that the men on the ground could see the hooks on either side of the plane's nose that would catch onto the nylon rope and guide it into the winch. The balloon jerked as the retrieval gear snapped onto the nylon rope. The rope was cut and the balloon broke away, drifting upward. The package of electronic gear was jerked off the ground as if it had been shot from a gun. In seconds it was accelerating into the sky as the winch quickly reeled in the line.

Yermolav silently watched the Sky Hook plane pick up the fire control equipment he had worked so hard to salvage. Even though he was their prisoner, he had to admire these Yankees. This Captain Reese had completely outwitted Vinh and his Vietnamese infantry, and this balloon retrieval of the equipment from deep inside enemy territory was a stroke of genius. From what he had seen of the two armies there was no way the Americans could lose this war. Unless, of course, their fainthearted, corrupt politicians prevented the Army from winning.

This was the one thing he had never understood about the Americans. The United States had the military and industrial strength to crush North Vietnam totally, but they didn't have the national will to do it. He had seen the disastrous results of the vaunted North Vietnamese Tet Offensive against the South. The North Vietnamese had been soundly defeated. But between the so-called free press and the cowards in the American Congress, a decisive victory had been turned into a crushing defeat.

After he had seen what a democratic government had done to the American Army, Yermolav wasn't sure he wanted to have any part of it. The Soviet system had its problems, he had to admit that, but at least it didn't betray the men who fought and died for it.

The second load of equipment went as smoothly as the first, and it was time to send Jones. The wounded man was drifting in and out of consciousness, and Reese radioed his condition. The Sky Hook pilot told him they would help Jones on board and that they had a medic with them. The C-130 made another pass, and

Jones was snatched off the ground as quickly as the equipment had been.

As soon as he was clear, Kegan's balloon was released.

"Good luck, Sergeant," Reese said.

"Thanks a lot, Captain." Kegan held out his hand. "I really owe you guys a big one, and if there's anything I can ever do for you, all you have to do is ask."

Reese shook his hand warmly. "You just get back in one of those fancy-ass gunships and kill as many of those bastards as you can. Every one you can kill on the Trail is just one more I don't have to kill somewhere in the jungle later."

"You've got my word on that, sir."

"Good luck, Sergeant."

"It looks like you're next, Nails," Reese said as soon as Kegan was in the air.

Hammer looked apprehensively at the quickly filling helium balloon. "Did I ever mention to you that I get airsick a lot?"

Reese grinned. "Sorry about that. But this is the fastest way to get you outta here."

"Look," Hammer said as he watched the balloon rise into the sky, "if you should ever get up my way, the Sixteenth Special Operations Squadron at Udorn, you be sure to drop in. I owe you at least a drink or two."

"If I'm ever up that way," Reese said, smiling, "I'll stop by. You can count on that. But you're not going to get away with just a couple of drinks, you cheap bastard. It's also going to cost you one of those famous Air Force steaks."

Hammer grinned. "You can have all the fucking steaks you can eat."

"I'll hold you to that."

The balloon reached the end of the line as the Sky Hook plane completed its turn and lined up for the snatch. "Get ready," Reese warned. "Now!"

Hammer was jerked off the ground as if he had been tied to a rocket. A thin scream followed him all the way up.

Reese watched as the Sky Hook plane flew out of sight before calling in the successful completion of the mission. Now it was time to see about getting his people back home.

Making a quick call back to Black Snake Three, Reese arranged for a Jolly Green Giant to come into a PZ a few klicks to the south. None of his Nungs was wounded seriously enough to need immediate evacuation, and since it would take a while for the chopper to get to them, Reese didn't want to hang around the airfield. It was better to keep on the move in case anyone came to investigate the battle.

Giving the handset back to Torres, he turned to Santelli. "Snow's sending a Jolly Green for us, so let's get this area policed up so we can move out."

The packing for the Sky Hooks and the ammunition resupply was quickly stacked up to be burned before they moved out. The five helium bottles were wired with explosives for demolition, as well. Reese wasn't about to leave anything behind that might be of use to the enemy.

"What are you going to do about him?" Pierce asked, hooking a thumb toward the Russian prisoner.

Reese smiled. "I'd like to take him back with us. He'd be the first Russian we've ever captured, but that might be more trouble for us than it would be worth."

"What do you mean, sir?"

"You have to remember, Sarge. This is an unauthorized mission. If we come back with a Russian officer in tow, MACV is going to put my ass in a sling for creating a diplomatic incident."

"So," Pierce repeated, "what are you going to do with him? Shoot him?"

Reese grinned broadly. "No, I'm going to let him go."

Pierce was speechless for a moment. "You've got to be shitting me, sir! You can't just let him go!"

"Why not?" Reese said calmly. "This guy's not really a player in this war. We won't ever have to worry about him shooting at us again. He's little more than an aviation junk dealer, and we got our fire control gear back. Also, he did take out that Dink officer to protect those two airmen."

"But, sir, he's an enemy!"

"There are enemies and then there are enemies, Sarge." Reese chuckled. "As far as I'm concerned, MACV is a bigger threat to all of us than he is."

Pierce just shook his head slowly.

Yermolav watched Reese approach and wondered what an American prisoner of war camp would be like. So far he had to admit that the American commander had treated him fairly, but then Reese was a combat officer and had a soldier's sense of honor. The Americans in the rear areas might not treat him as well, but at least he wouldn't be in a North Vietnamese prison camp. He had seen the way the North Vietnamese treated captured Yankee flyers, and it made him sick to his stomach.

"Major," Reese announced, "I'm going to let you go. If you wait here, someone will come to get you before too long. There is food and water in the buildings, and you should be able to manage until you're rescued."

Yermolav wasn't sure he understood the American correctly. "You are not going to take me back with you?"

Reese shook his head. "No. You're free to go. I owe you one for having protected those two men."

When Yermolav realized what Reese was saying, he snapped to attention and rendered a sharp salute. "Thank you, Captain."

Reese came to attention and returned the Russian officer's salute. "Good luck, Major. I hope you make it back."

Yermolav smiled. "And you also, Captain. Good luck and have a safe journey."

"Okay," Reese said, shrugging his shoulders to settle his ruck, "let's get humping. It's three klicks to our PZ."

Bolan goes head to head with a renegade dictator.

DON PENDLETON's
MACK BOLAN®

What civilization has feared most since Hitler is about to
happen: deadly technology reaching the hands of a madman.
All he needs to complete his doomsday weapon is a missing
scrambler component. But there is a major obstacle in his
way—The Executioner.

Mack Bolan's mission: intercept the missing component and
put an end to a bloody game of tag with fanatical cutthroats.

A storm is brewing in the Middle East and Mack Bolan is there in . . .

THE STORM TRILOGY

Along with PHOENIX FORCE and ABLE TEAM, THE EXECUTIONER is waging war against terrorism at home and abroad.

Be sure to catch all the action of this hard-hitting trilogy starting in April and continuing through to June.

Available at your favorite retail outlet, or order your copy now:

Book I:	STORM WARNING (THE EXECUTIONER #160)	$3.50	☐
Book II:	EYE OF THE STORM (THE EXECUTIONER #161)	$3.50	☐
Book III:	STORM BURST (352-page MACK BOLAN)	$4.99	☐

Total Amount	$ _____
Plus 75¢ Postage ($1.00 in Canada)	_____
Canadian residents add applicable federal and provincial taxes.	
Total Payable	$ _____

Please send a check or money order payable to Gold Eagle Books to:

In the U.S.
3010 Walden Avenue
P.O. Box 1325
Buffalo, NY 14269-1325

In Canada
P.O. Box 609
Fort Erie, Ontario
L2A 5X3

Please Print:

Name: _____

Address: _____

City: _____

State/Province: _____

Zip/Postal Code: _____

GOLD EAGLE ●

ST92-1